THE MADDY SAGA

BOOK FIVE

I0525726

PONYGIRL LOVE

BY

PAUL BLADES

Cover Art by Agnes Knox
agnesknox@simonas.se
agnes.knox@gmail.com

Copyright©2010 Paul Blades

Dark Visions Publications
darkvisionspub@gmail.com

All characters and events portrayed in this work are
fictitious

Previously published:

Watch for publication of the other books in the Maddy Saga:

Other books by Paul Blades:

Klitzman's Isle
Klitzman's Empire
Klitzman's Paradise
Klitzman's Pawn Part One
Klitzman's Pawn Part Two
The Taking of Cheryl Part One
The Taking of Cheryl Part Two: Slaver's Bait
Comfort Girl No. 4
Sacrifice to the Emerald God
The Blue Cantina: Anna's Surrender
The Warlord's Concubine
Dreams and Desires

All rights reserved. No part of this book may be reproduced, stored in a retrieval system, or transmitted in any form by any means including mechanical, electronic, photocopying, recording or otherwise without the express written permission of the publisher.

CHAPTER ONE
A TRIP THROUGH THE WOODS

Ponygirl summer was over. Not that the heat and the beautiful weather didn't continue right up until late September, but as of August 1, the 'vacation' for the racing ponygirls was spent. It was time to begin preparations for the fall racing season.

Lightning had enjoyed the leisurely, almost carefree days. Her time was mostly divided between casual turns around the practice track, laconic intervals in the ponygirl pasture with her sister ponies and fucking.

She lived for the fucking. Everything else had been taken away from her but her ability to experience physical pleasure. She could not speak. She could not use her arms, which were constantly bound behind her. She could make no decisions about what she would do or when she would do it. She had no remaining volitional abilities, unless you included her ability to decide to obey. This was technically a choice that she had to make a hundred times a day. But she had experienced such a multitude of thrashings and other punishments that disobedience had been erased from her mind as an option. If she had been told to run off of the top of a cliff into molten lava, she would have been unhappy, but refusal would not have crossed her mind.

But the fucking, that was something else. She had, at first, inwardly resisted the men's callous use of her. Somehow, though, within a very few days of her beastly conversion, her passions had begun to overflow whenever one of the masters' coarse, demanding hands stroked the soft, bare lips of her pudendum. She would fight it, but the men knew what they were doing. As she stood helpless in her stall, her new nose ring tethered to the wall in front of her, her ankles spread wide and anchored to the floor, her belly forced up against the beam that ran across her solitary hell, strong, hot hands would take hold of her breasts from behind, stroking, massaging them, pinching and twisting her nipples until she could fight off the arousal no more. Thick, rigid, anonymous cocks would find their way to her moistening slit and, once they gained entry, would ride her slowly, steadily until her knees buckled and she moaned through her remorseless gag. When she came, she snorted and groaned, her body trembling as the unknown assailant spilled his hot cream into her depths. It was not long before she would yearn for one of the men to possess her, to bring her the only joy of which she was now capable.

Lightning, the former Madeline Burnham, was a 21st century anomaly. She had once been a free, light hearted, liberated American woman of 19 years of age. But that time seemed centuries ago. Maddy had been kidnapped and brought to the former Soviet Republic of Kalikastan to be transformed into a half beast, half woman. Her head had been shaved except for the long, auburn colored ponytail that had been left in place. She was kept naked and bound, her face wholly obscured by a blue, neoprene hood with only tiny, dime sized outlets for her vision, erasing all traces of individuality. Her mouth was continuously filled with either a thick, leather gag covered by a broad leather shield that obscured the lower portion of her face, or a leather wrapped, steel bit attached to a cruel, steel plate that depressed her tongue. Her nether lips were kept as hairless as the day she was born and two small, golden disks imprinted with the details of her ownership dangled there.

On her chest, above her sizeable breasts, she wore, tattooed in large, blue, Cyrillic letters, her pony name, '*Molnya*', 'Lightning' in Russian. It was a name that she had accepted, her human one seeming quaint and archaic now taking into account her new circumstances, her new life. On her lower belly, just above her hairless mons, she was marked with an 8" high, bright yellow tattoo of a rampant wolf, its fangs snarling, its paws lifted in assertion of its ferocity. This was the heraldic symbol that had been adopted by her training stable and owner, Axmail Grobgy, a notorious Russian crime lord. Underneath the horrific portrait of the angry wolf was imprinted the motto of the estate, 'Sub Hoc Signo Vinces' - Under This Sign We Shall Conquer.

Lightning's owner was a former NKVD sergeant who had risen in the world since the collapse of the 'evil empire'. He ran much of the smuggling of drugs and other contraband to and from the newly independent Russian and Ukrainian Republics. Kalikastan was strategically nestled in the crux of those two much larger nations. It was a haven for the criminal element from both countries, a sort of Wild West of the East. The country was run by a "Commission" consisting of representatives of the major criminal clans. In its small but powerful offices in the capital, Dlitski, it settled clan disputes, maintained the tightly sealed borders (sealed from outsiders that is) and kept the modicum of actual governmental obligations to a minimum.

Grobgy, like several dozen of the more successful pirates of the new former Soviet 'democracies', had purchased the grounds of a defunct collective farm in the Kalikastan hinterland and turned it into a baronial estate. He tenanted out many of the old wheat fields and erected a fine mansion. Since they were reviving the feudal customs of the past, it was a small step to bring back the classic sport of ponygirl racing. Young, tall, well built, shapely women, mostly from Europe and North America, were kidnapped, dehumanized and trained to pull and race a ponycart.

Lightning had been recruited at the beginning of the spring racing season. She had been what was called a 'yearling', a pony in its first racing year. But now she was much more than that. Lightning had been moved from hauling a two pony cart as part of a yearling team to the single pony division of the 1500 meter sulky. And she had flowered into one of the fastest ponies on two feet. She had come away from the Spring Tournament as a champion. She now wore a golden medal attached to her ponygirl collar to prove it. It was something that Lightning was proud of. If she had to be a ponygirl, she wanted to be among the best.

At first, like all the other ponygirls, Lightning had rebelled against the grotesque life to which she had been condemned. She had been callously raped time and time again, pierced and permanently marked. She yearned to cry out and beg for her freedom, for mercy, to ask where she was and what was to become of her. She spent countless hours bound and alone in her ponygirl stall, railing against her cruel fate. But time, brutality and continuous indifference to her humanity had driven thoughts of redemption deep down inside her. She had become resigned to the daily use of her body by the men who dominated her. She had grown indifferent to the uselessness of her hands which were bound to a strap that descended from the back of her ponygirl collar. She had lost the will to speak, except to scream and plead from behind her gag wordlessly when she was beaten, or to cry out her pleasure when she was used.

The aim of ponygirl training was to create a totally sensual being, a creature interested only in the exquisite immediacy of the now. Nothing was explained to a ponygirl, nothing was said to her except for a small number of curt commands. Her thoughts of herself as a human person were to be totally crushed. The experience of total sexual subjugation, being brought to orgasm, minimally, several times per day, was designed to increase the new pony's awareness of her physical self, her body's animalistic needs. That and running, running, running.

And so, Maddy had become Lightning, had done her best to suppress her memories of her former self. She learned to race a ponycart around the track, learned to spread her lips and her legs for her masters, had learned to yearn for the delight of her use, to need it, as a pet needed the caress of its owner.

The surprising delight of her summer interlude had been her rapprochement with her original trainer, Anton Drabik. Drabik, a former Soviet Army colonel who had made his bones in Afghanistan, was Grobgy's chief hatchet man. He had left a trail of bodies behind him from Sevastopol to St. Petersburg, and from Kiev to Kamatchka. He was also a brutal and efficient trainer of ponygirls. He had many successful racers including eight champions to his credit. The latest was Lightning. He had named her that when she first came to the Grobgy estate and come under his thrall. He had spotted her as a potential champion right away. Her physique, tall and muscular, but well proportioned and shapely, was ideal for a ponygirl. After a while, he had found himself falling into a spell of obsession for this American ponygirl, a spell he had tried desperately to break.

But since the beginning of ponygirl summer, he had come to accept his special need for this pony's physical affections. He saw her now almost daily, usually in the evenings when the ponygirls were mounted in their pony stalls, posed for their masters' pleasures, awaiting the deepening of the dark to be bound and chained to the floor for the night. The ponies would be stood up, facing the back of their stalls, their black booted ankles spread and chained to rings in the floor. Their waists would be pressed up against the wooden bar that ran across the front of their five by seven foot stall, and the brass rings in their noses tied off to the wall in front of them, pulling them forwards, arching their backs and making their hairless sexes available for use.

Tied off in her stall, her nose ring chained taut to the wall, Lightning could not turn and see who came in to use her. But she had learned to listen for the distinctive tread of her trainer's boots. And he always greeted her in the same way, by drawing a long, thick finger along the hairless slit of her sex from behind.

Sometimes, he would take her right there, just as she was, plowing her musky channel, driving her to orgasm before spilling himself in the narrow, sensitive passage of her rear. He had taught the ponygirl to relish the use of her little brown star. She would moan with desperate pleasure as he rasped his stiff cock along the tender skin of its entrance.

Other nights, Drabik would release the desirable, young pony and, guiding her to her knees, allow her to express her affection for him with her plump, agile lips. On nights when his passion was raw, he would lay her down on the floor of her stall, strip himself naked, and ride her like the beast that she was.

When he could, in the late afternoons, Drabik harnessed Lightning and her ponygirl lover, Persephone, whom she had raced with as a yearling, and drove them over the narrow, shaded country roads that surrounded the estate. There was a spot about three miles out where he would stop and unhitch the ponies and, after watering them, remove their bits and allow them to make love to each other in the silken grass. It was a bucolic location. A meandering brook led to a small pond. There was a tall chestnut tree that drew a canopy over the amorous activities. When he thought that they had had enough, he would fuck one of them while the other happily watched.

Ironically, it was this very activity that led to the only dark spot of the summer for Lightning. Drabik had been called away on assignment for several days. His activities with the ponygirl Lightning had been carefully watched by Grobgy's beautiful but depraved daughter, Anya. She and Drabik were lovers. They had to hide it from her father since he disapproved of his daughter taking male lovers. She was allowed to use the ponies or the female slaves as much as she wanted. But Grobgy didn't want any of the help fucking his daughter, something that more than one man had learned to his fatal dismay.

It was Anya who had driven Drabik to torture and abuse Lightning some months ago, just before she had been assigned to a driver for the racing season. The tall, black haired woman had egged Drabik on and watched while he mercilessly abused her, hoping to drive out his obsession with her. It had worked for a while, and when Lightning was returned to the stables when the spring racing season was over, Drabik had taken Lightning to a remote location on the estate and beat her until she was senseless. But he found that it had only primed his lust for the luscious, shapely pony and he had made his peace with her. He still fucked Anya in their hideaway at an inn several miles from the estate, but Anya begrudged him the times that he spent with his ponygirl whore. And with Drabik gone, she decided to do something about it.

Lightning was not surprised to be hitched into a team with her ponygirl friend and lover, Persephone. She had never seen her face, but recognized her body, the thick, pendulous breasts and the Cyrillic spelling of her name tattooed over her chest. Waiting for Drabik to arrive, she rubbed her naked shoulder against the other's as they stood, relishing the warmth of her skin and anticipating a sensuous interlude with her. She felt, but did not see, a driver mount the light cart behind them. The eyes of the neoprene hoods that the naked ponygirls wore were tiny, dime sized holes. Their sight was extremely limited. They saw just as much as they needed to see and no more. Their leather covered, hard, plastic collars held their chins up at an angle. When tied off to a cart, the blue hooded ponies were forced to stare straight ahead as the reins that led from their harsh bits to the cart were always kept quite tight, preventing them from turning their heads.

There was a tug on the reins, the signal to go into motion, and the two hooded and naked ponygirls took off obediently in a little trot.

Lightning knew that something was wrong right away. She was, by now, a very experienced ponygirl and she was very sensitive to the weight she was pulling. Anya, of course, was lighter than Drabik and so the pony became aware almost immediately that it was not her trainer that was driving. Also, every driver had his own 'hand', so to speak, a handling style, and as the ponies made a turn to trot down the long driveway that led away from the mansion, the feel on her reins was not quite right.

But ponygirls were trained to questionless obedience and so the two ponies marched on without hesitation. It was not left up to ponygirls who would use them. Once they had cleared the estate driveway, the reins tugged again and the ponies broke into a lope. After a hundred or so yards, the reins were jiggled once more and the ponies began to sprint.

Ponygirl training paid careful attention to acclimating the ponies to orders conveyed to them through their reins. Verbal commands were always kept to an absolute minimum. This was especially important on race days when the roar of the crowds who assembled to enjoy the strange spectacle of former women hauling carts and carriages around a racing track at breakneck speeds could drown out any shouted command. Similarly, during training, ponygirls were sometimes made to run with the Velcro flaps over their small eye holes closed. They learned to take the turns of the track literally in complete darkness. Only by assiduous compliance with the demands of the reins could they avoid crashing into a rail. Thus, during a race, even though they raced with their eyes opened, they would respond instantly and automatically to any direction from their rider.

Lightning and Persephone quickly got into the rhythm of their sprint. They had raced together for half a season before Lightning was moved up to the sulkies, and it seemed like old times to them. What did it matter who had taken them out for a spin after all?

But the sprint went on and on. Lightning and Persephone were used to 1500 meter sprints, the length of the races they ran. And they had been limited to light workouts ever since the season had ended. This distance was much further and the back and leg muscles of the sweating, straining ponies began to tire. Mere physical exhaustion would not stop them, however. Unless their handler eased up on the reins, they would run until they dropped. Finally, after a run of over three miles, when they reached the shaded glen where they had spent so much pleasurable time with Drabik, the reins were pulled back, bringing the ponies to a sharp halt.

Lightning and Persephone were heaving heavily, gasping for air, when their rider came around to greet them. When Lightning saw who it was, her blood froze. She knew this cruel woman, although she didn't know her name. She had guessed that she was her trainer's lover. Looking into the cruel face of the beautiful, black haired woman, she knew that she was now going to have to pay the piper for her passion filled dances with him.

The lithe, pale skinned woman smiled as she saw the breathless ponies before her. She was wearing tight black, leather pants, a white blouse and high, black leather boots. Her long, black hair ran loosely down her back. Her eyebrows were trimmed in a thin arch above her eyes and she was wearing a dark, red lipstick. She grabbed the nipples of Lightning's breasts and shook her plump mounds, pinching them tightly, making her moan. She spoke to the ponygirl in English, something that was never done.

"Do you like fucking my lover, whore?" she said sternly. Lightning was shocked to hear words spoken in her former language. Persephone was too, and her head perked up. Persephone was a former student at UCLA. She had no idea that Lightning, her companion, was American, what her original name was or, of course, what she looked like under her permanent hood of blue. But now, at least, she knew that she spoke English.

"Cat got your tongue, *Molnya*?" the menacing female asked her. She put a special emphasis on the word '*Molnya*' as if to highlight the dehumanizing aspect of the name. As she spoke, she twisted Lightning's nipples harshly. The frightened ponygirl's wince was hidden by her hooded face, but her short intake of breath betrayed her.

Before releasing Lightning from her traces, Anya attached a thin rope to the golden ring that dangled from her nose. So when the ponygirl was freed from the cart, she was still under the cruel woman's control. "Come with me, *Molnya*," she said, tugging on her ring. "We are going to have a little fun."

Anya pulled the docile, naked, bound and blue hooded pony over to the large tree that dominated the glade. She took the other end of the rope and she tossed it over a tall, heavy branch that pushed out from the tree. She tied the free end to the ring in the front of Lightning's collar, pulling it tight, causing Lightning's head to lean back and her face to point at the heavy foliage above her. Lightning was forced to her tip toes to assuage the pressure on her septum. The woman walked away from her and when she returned, Lightning felt her legs being moved. Anya had found a long, thick branch that had fallen to the ground and she lashed Lightning's boots to it, forcing her to spread her legs widely and putting more of her weight on her already throbbing nose. Lightning whined with pain. She was only just able to keep the very tips of her heavy, black leather boots on the ground.

Suspended helplessly, her eyesight limited to what she could see directly above her, Lightning heard the sounds of her sister pony and lover being unhitched from the cart. She trembled with fear for her lover. The pony was led to a spot in the grass about twenty feet away from where Lightning was bound and forced to kneel before her. Persephone was smart enough to know that something special was about to happen. She had seen the dark haired beauty before, riding her tall, white thoroughbred or leading another ponygirl away from the barn for illicit purposes. But this was the first time that she had seen her up close and she shuddered at the cruelty she saw in her eyes.

Anya clipped Persephone's ankles together by the rings in her boots. If Persephone was going to run, she would have to hop away.

Anya came back to her other helpless prisoner. She took in the amusing sight of the naked, blue headed pony straining to ease the tension on her nose, her heavy, bare breasts swaying to and fro. There was no temptation for her to think of the unhappy creature as a woman. Her prominent tattoos, the rings through her nose and labia, and the featureless face were evidence enough that all of that had been taken away from her. But it pleased the vengeful young woman to remind the pitiful ponygirl of what she once was. Nothing, not even the whip, could be crueler.

"I hear that you and Persephone are lovers, *Molnya,*" she asked Lightning tauntingly. "Is this true?" She was standing behind the unhappy pony and caressing her heavy breasts, whispering into her ear. She tugged and pulled at the thick nipples until they were hard. She was about the same height as the ponygirl and she placed her lips on Lightning's throat and suckled at it, drawing an unwanted moan from her.

Satisfied at the sound that she had driven from the pony, she lifted her head from her neck. "Of course she is," Anya continued. "You don't have to tell me. I've been watching you." She ran her hands down Lightning's taut belly and along the inside of her stretched thighs. "You shouldn't get emotionally involved with another pony, *Molnya.* After all, you're just an animal now. And animals don't have feelings, do they?"

The cruel pirate's daughter grabbed Lightning's hairless nether lips and pinched them tightly. Lightning squirmed as the pain coursed through her, a motion that brought agony to her stretched septum. "I don't know if you will be sorry today that you fell in love with her, but I can assure you that she will be," Anya snarled. "You've bewitched my lover to satisfy your pleasures and so I'm going to use your lover to satisfy mine. I can assure you that my lusts are not quite so benign as yours."

Lightning quailed as she contemplated the cruelties that were about to be inflicted on her friend. Whipping and punishment were a daily part of ponygirl life, and any pony could be singled out for a beating any day for any reason. But Lightning knew that this woman intended that something more than an ordinary thrashing be imposed on her lover. She tried to beg through her bit for mercy from the evil woman, but the sounds she made were unintelligible. Anya rubbed her hand along Lightning's exposed throat. "No talking, ponygirl," she said, laughing.

The sound of ponygirls boots at the run reached Lightning's ear, at first faintly, and then as they came closer, louder and louder. She heard a cart being pulled to a stop not far from where she stood. "Ah," Anya said in a self satisfied tone, "my helpers have arrived."

Two heavy set, sturdy stable boys leapt off of the seat of a six pony cabriolet. Three rows of panting, naked, blue hooded ponygirls stood in front of it snorting and straining for air. Before walking over to the small glade, the stable boys, men really, placed hobbles on the feet of the two lead ponies. It was doubtful that they would run away of their own accord, but why take chances?

Persephone had turned her head when she heard the pony carriage come near and she watched through the small eyelets in her blue hood as the men approached. She had heard Anya's taunting words and her stomach began to churn with fear. The men were carrying an assortment of whips in their hands.

With the presence of the men, Anya ceased speaking directly to her pony captive and spoke Russian to the men. "There she is," she said, pointing at the kneeling ponygirl. "Have some fun with her."

Lightning heard Anya speak to the men, and she heard their amused replies. Anya took up her position behind the distraught ponygirl and, with her hands on her curvaceous hips, whispered in her ear. "I've asked Sergi and Pavlov to take your little friend in hand, ponygirl. Let's listen to them give her a good lesson in ponygirl discipline."

When Lightning heard the first crack of the whip, she gave out a piteous whine. She had caused Persephone to be whipped once before, when, at the beginning of a race she had slipped and fell, bringing Persephone down with her. Their driver had punished them both. She had felt dolefully guilty for days for bringing pain to her lover. But those blows had been imposed by a man who had reason to restrain his vilest impulses. He was responsible for them, wanted them to race for him. And afterwards, he had forgiven them. But Lightning sensed that these men were under no such restraints.

The strung up ponygirl flinched when she heard the first angry lash kiss her lover's flesh. Persephone screamed through her bit. Again and again the whips landed, each time followed quickly with a distorted, anguished, female cry of pain. Lightning yearned to take in the brutal spectacle of her lover's torture, not because it would assuage her torment in any way, but because she felt drawn to it like a spectator to a horrible fire.

As the terrorized pony wailed and screamed at the application of the whips to her defenseless body, Anya pressed her body up against Lightning's and tormented the pony with her hands. She massaged the pony's swollen breasts, teased the stiff, blood filled nipples. She kissed her neck and under her chin, dragging her hot tongue across her flesh. And then she lowered her hands, gently stroking the tight skin across her belly, until they reached the apex of her spread thighs and seized her tender nether lips.

There was no way for Lightning to know how many men had handled her body since she had become a ponygirl. She guessed that it was dozens, if not more. Day after day, she had been trained to respond passionately to the manipulation of her sex, hands against her flesh, the massage of her tender orbs. Whether it was the unleashing of a substrata of licentiousness that had always been there beneath her cultured, demure exterior, or due to the poisoning of her soul, creating a burning need for satisfied lust, Lightning now responded almost immediately whenever hands or lips stoked her passions. She had no choice now but to let the hands of her cruel mistress enflame her. She cursed herself as her blood rose, even as her ears received the long, plaintive cries of her soul mate.

Anya watched feverishly as the men trammeled the other pony with their whips. They had laid her across a fallen tree trunk, facing the sky and were lashing her repeatedly with fierce, intense strokes. Dark, angry blotches of red had broken out all over her breasts and belly as well as the tops of her thighs. Her legs had been spread apart and when the lashes struck the hairless, distended labia, and delved into the tender slit between them, Persephone's anguished cries reached a new crescendo.

Lightning began to cry and wail even as her passions were being driven to their heights. She could not witness the torment of her lover, but she recorded every crack of the whips, every moan and cry of pain. She was ashamed that she could experience pleasure while her sister pony was being so cruelly tortured and she closed her eyes shut tightly and bit down on the leather covered steel bar in her mouth in supreme frustration and remorse. But the demands of the hand that stroked her flowered sex were insistent. Anya had one hand buried deep in Lightning's moist, loose pussy and one hand on the pony's breasts, teasing and tormenting them. Soon, the sounds of her lover's torture began to be drowned out by the rush of her own lust. Her hips involuntarily shook as Anya tickled the tiny bud of pleasure atop her leaking canal. She moaned when the woman's fingers captured it and massaged it until she could not restrain her response. Lightning cried out as her pussy's spasms began, calling out at each strong, hard contraction.

"Come, little ponygirl, come!' Anya yelled into her ear. "Come while you lover feels the fiery bite of the whips that you brought to her!"

Lightning's crushing throbs grew more intense at the encouragement of her mistress. Ironically, she felt that she was punishing herself for bringing such pain and torment to her lover. Each mind crushing pulse of her pussy's walls brought a wave of deep guilt that passed through her like a viscous poison.

Anya made Lightning climb the mountain a second time. The pony shook her hips and tried to twist her body away, but it brought only mind numbing pain to her through the ring in her nose. Her legs ached from being stretched; her feet were cramped and painful. But the manipulation of her tender sex continued to drive her desire. By the time that her second orgasm came crashing through her, she was attempting to capture the torturous hand on her sex between her shuddering thighs

As Anya let her prisoner's lusts cool, she signaled the stable boys to begin the next phase of Perephone's ordeal. They released her from the tree trunk and dragged her to within ten feet of the strung up ponygirl. Pushing her to her knees, her forehead to the ground, the men spread open her thighs and then one after the other raped her cruelly and brutally.

Lightning could hear the anguished moans of her friend and the grunts of the stable boys directly in front of her. Anya casually stroked the pony's naked lower lips as she watched. "Your friend can really take a cock," she whispered to the dangling ponygirl as one of the stable boys pressed his prick deep into the supine ponygirl's throat. Lightning could hear Persephone gag and whine for air as the men laughed.

Finally, the men were through with her. Persephone lay in the grass moaning her unhappiness and residual pain. Lightning was crying with helpless misery at the hell that she had caused to be visited on her friend. But Anya was not finished.

The black haired woman ordered the men to hitch Persephone back up to the cart. Once the men had remounted their carriage and gone on their way, she disappeared for a moment into the woods. She came out a few moments later, carrying a long, thin branch of a sticker bush. She peeled away the leaves on it together with the largest, sharpest thorns with a small penknife. When she was satisfied with it, she brought it over to where Lightning was still bound.

"Feel this, ponygirl," she taunted as she dragged the pricker covered branch between Lightning's thighs. Lightning stiffened with pain as the small, sharp thorns raked her tender flesh. "I'm going to whip you with this, whore," Anya told her, her voice filled with hatred and cruelty. "I want you to remember this day well. The next time you have my lover's cock in your mouth, I want you to think of the price that you will be paying for it when I get you alone."

Anya swept the branch behind her and brought it forward with all her might. It struck Lightning across her pale, white breasts and the pony screeched with pain. She struck her across her tummy, her thighs, the sides of her arms. The angry, cruel, black haired woman went behind her and struck at the back of her legs, over her bound hands and wrists, across her naked back. She drew the length of the sharp, prickly branch between her thighs on either side of her soft, tender labia and up the crack between her rear globes. Again and again the fierce woman struck her, causing the poor ponygirl to dance and cry with pain.

Anya, out of breath from her exertions, finally tossed the branch aside. She undid Lightning's ankles and then untied the rope that had held the helpless pony up by her ringed nose. Lightning moaned with joy as she found her feet again and the agonizing pain in her nostrils subsided. Anya ordered her to her knees.

Holding the rope that was tied to Lightning's nose ring in one hand, Anya pulled off her boots and began to strip her tight, black leather pants from her legs. When they were off, she stepped out of her lacy black thong. Her pleasure lips were covered by a thick thatch of curly black hair. Her legs were pale and graceful. She backed herself up against the tree and pulled the ponygirl close to her. Lightning felt the woman's hands undo the straps from her bit and the offensive contrivance fell from her mouth. "Suck my cunt, whore," the woman told her, her voice cold as steel.

Lightning looked ahead of her through the tiny, dime sized holes in her hood and saw the spread legs of her tormentor. Through the wiry, black bush, she could see the outline of her lower lips and a tell tale glistening of arousal in the slit between them. Lightning wanted, with all of her heart, to bring intense pain to the woman who had caused her lover so much torment. She knew that she could tear off the cruel woman's tender love bud with her teeth if she wanted. She could cause this woman true agony. But she knew that she wouldn't. She could not imagine the torments that would be visited upon herself and her lover if she did. Besides, she knew that this cruel woman had all the right in the world to punish her for her transgressions. She was no longer a woman. She was a beast upon all was imposed and of whom nothing was asked. She had no rights, not even the right to love. Miserably, she bent her neck and shoulders and pushed her lips through the mass of curly black hair until she met the tender, hot love lips of her tormentor.

Anya looked down on the blood streaked back of the abject ponygirl. The sticker bush branch had torn a thousand small cuts into her flesh and small trails of blood oozed from them. When she felt the tongue of the pony spread her labial lips, she moaned with pleasure and satisfaction. The world had been returned to its rightful place. The ponygirl who had stolen her lover had paid the price for her sin. And she would pay again and again as long as the man who truly belonged to her was mesmerized by the ponygirl's flesh.

As Lightning's tongue and lips excited her sex, Anya began to moan with pleasure. She had her back against the thick oak tree and her legs were spread wide. Her hands rested on the blue clad head of the pony between her thighs and she rocked and thrust her hips as her passion began to build. Lightning's tongue played with her stiff clit, causing the tall, thin woman to shudder with delight. When she began to suck on it, Anya groaned with pleasure. As her pussy began to throb and convulse with the intense contractions of her climax, Anya yelled loudly and pressed the blue hooded head hard against her loins.

CHAPTER TWO
A USEFUL LESSON

"Seven and 10…seven and 15…seven and 20…seven and 25!"

The slightly built ponygirl trainer looked at his pocket watch in disgust. Seven minutes and twenty five seconds was nowhere near the time needed to finish in the first division during the Fall Tournament, never mind win the championship, and never mind smoking Lightning, Grobgy's 1500 meter sulky champion.

He watched while Chocolate was taken around the track in her cool down lap. Irkut was an experienced ponygirl trainer. He had trained some of the best. He had been in at the resurrection of the sport in Kalikastan over ten years ago and had made his fortune. Michael Burnham, the American millionaire, or rather multi, multi millionaire, had talked him out of retirement to train the dark brown pony to beat Lightning, last season's champion. At this speed, it would be lucky if they made the cutoff for the tournament.

Chocolate, the former Jackie Johnson, a 22 year old hooker from Chicago, had been recruited by Jake, Burnham's fixer, to challenge the ponygirl Lightning in a claiming race after the fall season. Lightning was actually Burnham's niece, Madeline Burnham, aka Maddy, who had been kidnapped by slavers six months ago, brought to the former Soviet Republic of Kalikastan, and converted to a ponygirl.

The search for Maddy had begun within a day of her kidnapping. Jake's team had traced her to a Georgia farmhouse where she had been held prisoner for a week or so and then to the basement of a uniform rental company warehouse in Elizabeth, New Jersey. The basement dungeon served as a way station for the team of slavers who had contracted for Maddy's capture. Jake had discovered that Maddy had been sent to Kalikastan. There was no way to trace her in that lawless country where female sexual slavery had been revived along with the ancient sport of ponygirl racing, and so Jake had concocted a scheme to take over the slavers' operations in the U.S. He would make contact with their customers in Kalikastan and Burnham would figure out a way to buy his way into the tightly sealed country.

Burnham dangled his company's ability to obtain a 20 billion dollar international pipeline contract that would go through Kalikastan. The opportunities for graft were enormous and in exchange for sharing the wealth, Burnham was granted honorary citizenship and the right to an estate where he could indulge in the country's favorite sport.

Jake, along with Irkut as his guide, had toured the many estates throughout the interior of the country hoping to spot Maddy. He got lucky and discovered that she was owned by Axmial Grobgy. Burnham, who had become enamored of the lifestyle of an owner of female slaves and ponygirls, had nixed a special ops mission to save Maddy. Grobgy, flush with Maddy's championship, had refused to sell her. Burnham's idea as he had explained it to Jake was to recruit their own star ponygirl and then wager the possibility of millions of dollars in graft with Grobgy in exchange for Maddy in a claiming race. If Maddy won, Grobgy got the illicit contracts and kept the ponygirl Lightning, as she was now called. If she lost, Burnham got to keep Maddy. Once they won her, the idea was to falsify her death and smuggle her out of the country. It was a highly risky scheme in which everything could go wrong. Grobgy still hadn't taken the bait. And Chocolate, the former Jackie Johnson, who had been recruited by Jake to challenge Lightning, was proving to be less than a stellar racer.

Chocolate had been promised a million dollars by Jake if she would submit to being a ponygirl for five months. She had been a high school track star back in Chicago before she took up 'the life' after a series of very bad decisions. Jake had saved her from a particularly nasty pimp and she was devoted to him. She was a tall, big boned girl with a natural grace and poise. Her large, delightful breasts and pleasing face had made her a first class whore. And her physique, desirable but strong and well toned, made her ideal to be recruited as a ponygirl.

The former call girl had taken hard to life as a ponygirl, which was much more oppressive than she had ever imagined. But, as Jake had warned her, in for a penny, in for a pound, and she was committed to this thing to the very end. Jake had told her that she would have to be a ponygirl for five months. It was more than a month now, and the hardened hooker still cried herself to sleep every night.

Ponygirls slept on the floor of the ponygirl barn, lying on their backs, their hands still bound behind them. They wore their thick, leather gags through the night and their feet and neck were anchored to the floor. The Velcro flaps on their hoods were closed, blocking out all light. It was a time of intense reflection for the ponygirls. The ponygirl barn was a lonely place at night, the only sounds being the rustling of other ponygirls' chains as they squirmed in place, the hard footfalls of the boots of the night watchman. The former women lay there, prisoners of their own bodies, unable to scratch their nose, roll over, sit up. On occasion, a trainer or a stable boy would come into the barn late at night and select a ponygirl for use. Her moans of pleasure, or pain, and the grunts of the man's lust would echo throughout the barn, a stark reminder to the rest of the ponies of their helpless state and their servile nature.

It was during this time that the ponygirls often thought of their former lives. They had all been plucked from their homelands, removed form their full and rich existences. Very few of them had any idea where they were. As far as they knew, no ponygirl had ever escaped. For the older ponies, these reflections on the past were intensely unwelcome and were driven from their minds as soon as possible. They had a new life now, one they had taken great efforts to adjust to. They wanted no thoughts of the past, or the future, to intrude on the delicate balance between acceptance and insanity that they had developed over many months or years.

But for the new ponies, it was hard. Only time would inure them to their new existence. Time and the whip. Jackie had been a pony for less than a month and bemoaned the loss of her personality. She knew that she stood out from all of the other ponygirls. She was the only brown skinned female among them. But the mere fact that she was instantly identifiable did not substitute for the expression of real personality. As a whore, Jackie had been able to let it all hang out. She had had no shame at what she did. She reveled in the power that her eroticism had given her over the often nervous and timid johns she had serviced. And the men who knew how to use a whore made her feel ennobled in her beauty and sensuality. The few that treated her meanly or even cruelly, she soon forgot. Since she had no pimp, she could pick and choose her tricks and anyone who failed to appreciate her charms and skills she dropped.

Since she had become a ponygirl, all that had changed. Men used her bodily orifices without even the slightest concession to her humanity. She could not control their passions, prolonging their groans and sighs of lust until they begged for relief, as she used to. Now, she was the one who begged for relief, although her moans and garbled exclamations could hardly be classified as words. Some of the men seemed to enjoy making her come, and she liked it too. She could hear them laugh and exclaim to each other in their strange tongue as she convulsed and spasmed in her passion. But most of them used her as a mere depository for their spunk, often leaving her writhing and shuddering with unfulfilled lust.

Bound at night, unable to move in any meaningful way, Jackie would bemoan her decision to become a dehumanized beast. She couldn't see how she could last for the five months that Jake had promised would be the limits of her captivity. She would twist and turn in miserable unhappiness. But then she would think of the money and what her life would be like free of all concerns. She would buy herself a house by the sea somewhere, California, or maybe Mexico where things were cheaper. She would get a piano, have flowers around her room all the time. She would live free from fear, of the police, of the johns, of disease and death. It would be wonderful. All she had to do was survive. She would run and run and run, as they were compelling her to do. She would even try her best at beating this other ponygirl when the big race came off. But either way, all she had to do was to survive and the money was hers. Jake had promised.

* * * * * * * * * *

Watching Chocolate trot slowly around the track after her test lap, Irkut knew he had a problem. He believed that Chocolate could be among the best. She had all the attributes. She had long, strong, sculpted legs, and a broad back. Her instincts were good and she was smart. After a shaky start, she had adjusted to pulling a cart. Her rebelliousness had been broken and she submitted enthusiastically to her use by the men. But there was something wrong. Something was holding her back. He couldn't figure it out.

In Jackie's mind, she was doing the best that she could. She thought that she was running fast each time that she was given a test run. But the whippings she received after every one told her different. She was beginning to despair of ever pleasing her cruel trainer. As she finished her cool down lap, she was brought even with where he was standing by the side of the track. She could see from his face that he was unhappy. She knew that she would be given five hard strokes of the riding crop on her buttocks. Her ass was sore almost every night that she went to bed. Her back was raw where her driver had whipped her, urging her on fruitlessly to greater speed.

The stable boy released Jackie from the harness and brought her over to a rail on the outside of the track. Jackie had been bent over it many times. He didn't have to tell her what to do. With a tear in her eye, she leaned over as the ring in her nose was attached by a chain to a ring in the ground. She felt her legs belted closely together.

Irkut took his time about administering the ponygirl's deserts. He rubbed his rough, gnarled hand over her sweaty flanks, appreciating the firm, smooth flesh. Jackie shuddered as she felt the rasp of the rough hand roll over her buttocks and drag along the outside of her thigh. She was bent in half over the rail. The rope that connected her nose ring to the peg in the ground was taut. Her plentiful breasts dangled down towards the ground and her rear was raised prominently. All she could see was a little patch of dusty earth in front of her through the tiny holes of her hood.

It was the humiliating confinements that Jackie hated most. She didn't mind the men looking at her body; she was used enough to that from her hooker days. But to be unable to brush away the hand that teased her breasts or to be tethered to a post like some dumb animal caused the anguish of her dreadful circumstances to well up inside. Jake had warned her when she was recruited. He said that it might be more than she could bear. She had not believed him then, but she did now. How many days did she have left as a ponygirl? She didn't know for sure, but she knew that it was a long time. Well, they wanted her to run, and run she would. But mostly she would endure. Whether she won the race against this other ponygirl was nothing to her. She wanted her million and to get out.

It was this lack of passionate need to excel that troubled Irkut. He didn't know its cause, but he had detected it. As he circled the wrinkled small entrance to Chocolate's bowels with his thumb, playing with it almost idly, he was deep in concentration. Jackie knew that she would spend some time bound over her post after her chastisement and that some of the men of this strange version of a horse farm would take advantage of her availability for use. The thick digit that teased her rear entrance caused her sex to involuntarily moisten. She had never permitted the use of this orifice to her clients. It was one of the few things that she wouldn't do. But since her reduction to the life of a pony, she had been forced to surrender it to the demands of the masters. She had been revolted, at first, and had screamed and yelled behind her gag as she was used, feeling the delicate flesh tear at the callous invasion. Since then, she had learned to accommodate the thick, anonymous members that pierced her there, and now she had even begun to feel sensual delight from the friction around the sensitive tissue that surrounded this portal. As Irkut's thumb teased this flesh, she felt an incipient desire rise within her. All of her consciousness was drawn to the possibilities suggested by the taunting finger, and the warmth that spread through her loins.

The trainer drew himself from his reverie. He knew what he would do. If it didn't work, he would wash his hands of her and advise Burnham to sell her off as a work pony somewhere. He didn't want his reputation tarnished by a lazy pony.

Irkut stood back and took the riding crop that he always kept dangling from his belt into his right hand. While the pony's rump was the most inviting target, the back of her thighs would inflict the most pain. He stepped back and brought the black leather crop down fiercely against the pony's flesh.

Irkut's transition from his pensive state to an active one happened so fast that Jackie had barely any time to prepare herself for the blow. The pain across her back legs was exquisite and her whole body stiffened as she absorbed it. She wailed behind her bit as the effects of the crop's fiery kiss coursed through her. As the crop came down again and again, she struggled to free her legs, tried to dodge the rain of blows. She knew that she was suffering for her failure to satisfy her trainer's demand for speed, but she was, she thought, running as fast as she could. But if she had to be whipped, so be it. She would take it, take it and endure. "Five months! Five months!" She repeated this mantra in her head even as her body absorbed the painful blows.

When Irkut had concluded his abuse of the helpless, brown skinned pony, he left her stretched across her rail while he went to make some preparations. A few of the stable hands had been patiently sitting on the fence, watching the administration of ponygirl discipline, and they hopped off when they saw Irkut walk away. There was a short argument over precedence, but shortly thereafter, the first of them presented his thick, hard cock to the little brown aperture. Jackie felt the man's hard hands spread her taut rear cheeks and the press of the bulbous head of his manhood against the small opening. The man made some humorous comment to his fellows and drooled a load of spit onto the end of his tool. It was all the lubrication she would get and Jackie prepared for the assault as she heard the men's taunting laughter.

"Mmmmmmmmmmmm!" Jackie moaned as the thick manhood spread her tender anus wide. She bucked her rear as she felt the long, hot cock enter her. Slowly, but surely, the shaft eased it way deeply inside her until it was buried to its hilt. Hot hands held onto the sides of her rump and she heard the man moan his delight. When he slowly drew his thick rod back and forth, Jackie, in spite of herself, reveled at the pleasurable friction of the cock along her rear's lips, delighted in the fullness of her bowel.

Once the man was assured that he could plough the ponygirl's back pathway with ease, he began a slow, steady stroke inside her. Jackie could feel her pussy tingle as the sensations of her filled rear communicated themselves to her sex. She twisted and turned her bound hands in a futile effort to ward off the pleasurable sensations. It was wrong, dirty and wrong, and she reviled herself for the pleasure she felt from it. "Auuuugh! Auuuuuuugh!" she called out through her bit, as she tried to beg the man to stop. Just as the sensations from behind her had reached their extreme, when she felt her lustful needs overwhelm her, she felt the man's leg muscles jam up against hers and tense and then heard the man grunt. He pounded her ass mercilessly as he came, slapping her exposed rear cheeks, spurting his copious load inside her.

And then, he withdrew. Jackie didn't know whether to be upset or glad. The pleasurable but tortuous rasping of the cock along the sensitive skin of her anal ring had stopped, but her pussy still burned with need. When the second man's cock addressed her entrance and began to slide past her distended ring of flesh, she moaned with anticipation.

The second man was quicker, and Jackie had just begun to feel her passion rising when he splashed his cum deep inside her, calling out his pleasure in a series of staccato moans. But the third man, she had no idea who he was, he was more patient. When the cock entered her, Jackie could tell right away that this was going to be different. The man played with the entrance to her bowels, thrusting the head of his hard wand of flesh past the burning lips and then out again.

Five, six, seven times, he pushed his cock past the now widened opening and withdrew it. Jackie was being driven mad with desire. She wanted this man's cock to penetrate her, to delve deeply within, to possess her. When the cock entered her the seventh time, she clamped her rear muscles around it as hard as she could and moaned her need. The man who was assaulting her laughed and called out to his fellows, who joined in the joke. Jackie felt humiliation flow through her but was unable to cool her passion. "Please, please, please," her mind begged.

Satisfied that he had stoked the helpless pony's need, the man began to fuck her ass in earnest. He took long, deep, steady strokes and listened for the ponygirl's lusts.

Jackie could feel her climax coming nearer and nearer. She wanted it so badly; she needed it. She tried to thrust back at the hips that pounded into her rear, but she had no slack in her distended body. Her breasts swayed and jerked, recording each hard thrust into her upraised rear. Finally, the ponygirl could feel the level of her lusts begin to overflow its banks. "Ooooooooooooh! Ooooooooooooooh!" she moaned through her clenched teeth. Despite her bindings, her body began to shake and quiver as her climax overtook her. The man snorted in triumph and began his own release, his hot cock pulsing and throbbing inside her.

Jackie was panting, her heart throbbing in her chest as the man slid his softening cock from within her. It was a first for her. Back in the day, she had heard from some of the other girls about the thrills of ass fucking, but had never believed it. Now she did.

The naked, brown ponygirl spent another hour bent over the rail before she was released by a stable boy and brought back into the pony barn for her lunch. Her back and thighs ached and her nose was sore, but she had endured her ordeal. Once she had entered her stall, the tall, blond haired young man brought her to her knees and fastened the back of her collar to a hook in the wall with a short chain. There was just enough room so that when he had returned with an earthenware bowl of mush for her to eat and removed her steel bit, she could bend down and lap up her lunch.

It had taken only a few days for Jackie to get used to eating from a bowl like a dog. Hunger is an ardent teacher. She had even learned to use her lips and tongue to slurp up her food without dirtying her tight, black hood, something she had been beaten for several times in the beginning. When the stable boy returned, he inserted her leather plug shield gag and helped her relieve her bladder and empty her bowels. He cleaned her and then mounted her in her stall to await her afternoon training session.

Standing alone in her stall, Jackie allowed her mind to drift into a dreamlike state. The background noises of the barn lulled her. She could still feel the widening of her rear entrance from the morning's rape. Her leg muscles were loose and mildly tired from her morning's exercise. She leaned her tattooed stomach against the railing that crossed her stall, easing the taut chain that connected her nose ring to the wall. Her black leather clad feet were spread widely, and fastened to rings in the floor, her wrists comfortably bound to the strap that hung from her collar behind her.

"Another day half done," she thought to herself. She tried to call into her mind her vision of her prospective, comfortable home overlooking the Pacific, imagining the sound of the crashing surf, the smell of the salt air. She swore that this ponygirl thing would all be a memory some day and that that would be her reality.

Jackie was startled out of her daydreams when the door to her stall opened behind her. She was released and she saw that it was her trainer who had come to get her. Taking the lead connected to her nose ring, he led her from the barn. Jackie had resolved to do as good as she could. Maybe if she ran just a little faster she could please the harsh man.

But the pony was not led to the track. A two pony cart was waiting outside the barn with two pale, heavyset, blond tailed ponies hitched to it. A well built, muscular man sat on the driver's seat expectantly. Irkut connected the chain from her nose ring to the back of the cart and walked away. There was a snap of reins and the ponycart took off. The hooded and bound, naked, brown skinned ponygirl was propelled quickly behind it.

The pace was a leisurely trot as the cart wound its way over the dirt pathway that led from the barn, along the track and past the woods on the other side. Jackie had never been this far away from the pony barn since she had arrived. She wondered with some trepidation where she was going. Although she had always assumed that she had been brought to the ponygirl estate that Jake had told her about, she hadn't seen or heard from him since her staged kidnapping. There was always a tinge of doubt in her mind, always the terrorizing prospect, too horrible to really contemplate, that somehow things had gotten messed up and she had been delivered to some other estate, to some other master and that she was condemned to be a ponygirl for real, forever. Her stomach fluttered as she recalled that possibility now. She knew that she had not pleased her trainer. What would be her fate if he gave up on her?

Once past the copse of trees that bordered the practice track, the dirt pathway entered a flat plain. The sides were bordered by tall, yellow grass, blowing gently in the mild, early August wind. The road was hot and dry, and the dirt kicked up by the ponygirls pulling the cart drifted up in a cloud of dust underneath and behind the cart. Jackie had no choice but to breathe in the fine particles and she coughed and sputtered as she followed helplessly. She could not see ahead of her beyond the rear of the cart and could only catch glimpses of the sides of the road through the tiny holes in her hood. To prevent the painful stress of the chain on her nose ring, she tried to keep a little slack in it, running closer to the rear of the cart than otherwise necessary, but that just increased the flow of choking dust over her face and so she gave it up, satisfied to allow a slight pressure on the large golden ring in her nose.

The steadily trotting pair of naked, blond tailed ponygirls, a filly in tow, and leading an old fashioned horse cart, made for a bucolic sight. The ease and nonchalance with which the driver held the reins, the obedient, natural gait of the lead ponies, the willingness of the brown skinned pony in the rear to allow herself to be led, all made the sight of the beastly, subservient, former women seem almost natural.

After a mile or so, the tall grass gave way on one side to a shortly cut, green and brown pasture bordered by a barbed wire fence. Chocolate could see and hear cows gathered here and there. The cart slowed as it entered a cluster of dark brown, wooden farm buildings. The dirt in the middle of the buildings was hard packed and there was a large, dirty, red panel truck parked next to the largest structure. A tall, wide girthed man wearing a white, blood stained apron emerged from the building through a wide, steel, roll up doorway. He was wiping his sweaty forehead with a dirty, damp cloth as he approached he cart. He exchanged a pleasantry with the driver and strolled slowly to the back. He had a large, closely shaven head and a well fed, jovial face. He looked upon Jackie's flesh admiringly. The chain linking Jackie to the cart had become slack and she tried to back away from the coarse, blood covered man as he reached out to grab her breast. His other hand took hold of the chain and reeled the frightened ponygirl closer to him.

Murmuring sweet sounding phrases, the man sized up Jackie's plump, right breast. He turned her around and ran his hand over her ample, firm rump and down over her thighs. He chuckled in a satisfied manner and then unhooked the chain from the back of the cart, keeping a hold on the other end of the chain close to Jackie's nose ring with his other hand. When the cart pulled away, making a wide circle to return to the estate, a wave of fear swept through the unhappy ponygirl.

A younger, thinner version of the fat man emerged from the large building. He had long, dirty blond hair that was bound to his head by a rolled up, faded, blue bandana. The fat man called something out to him and he went back inside only to emerge with a rolling framework. He brought it over to where Jackie and the fat man were standing. Jackie saw that the device had a series of rings and chains fastened to it and realized that it was for her. As the younger man wheeled it into position in front of her, Jackie's fear got the better of her and her bladder released, sending a torrent of pale yellow urine down her legs. Her knees went week and only the strong hand of the fat man holding the chain linked to her nose ring prevented her from collapsing to the ground.

The fat man stepped aside and laughed when he saw that the ponygirl had lost control of herself. He pulled her towards the cart, overcoming her feeble resistance and handed the chain to his assistant. Jackie whined with fear as she was forced to lean forward and her torso pushed down on a wide plank that ran across it. She felt her collar being affixed to a ring in the plank by the assistant while the fat man placed her knees in a kneeling position and fastened the rings in her boots to the floor. A thick, wide strap went around her waist, locking her in position.

The result was that Jackie was kneeling with her stomach and chest pressed against the board, horizontal to the ground. Her head was tilted up by the shape of her collar so that she could see in front of her. Her hips were slightly higher than her torso and her legs were spread, leaving her sex and rear vulnerable.

All kinds of things ran through Jackie's fevered mind as the cart was rolled towards the building. Maybe her trainer had given her to these men for the afternoon so that they could use her as some kind of punishment for her dismal performances. Maybe, like the first day that she had been here, the men were going to affix some new kind of piercing or marking on her. But the remote location and the appearance of the men, blood covered and dressed like her neighborhood butcher, drove a cold stake of terror through her heart.

When the cart was inside the building, after her eyes adjusted to the dimmer light, Jackie saw that her worst fears had been confirmed. A long rack of large, gleaming knives were lined up along the wall. A kind of track ran across the ceiling and towards a thick door with a handle like a refrigerator. But worst of all, dangling by two legs, blood seeping from its recently slashed neck into a tub underneath it was a large brown and white cow. Its legs were splayed widely and fastened to the track by chains around its ankles. The cow's thick, pink tongue dangled from its stilled mouth. Jackie began to whine and cry, bobbing her black clad head. Her whole body shook in the frame, but she was securely fastened. The men ignored her and went back to their work.

Many of the larger estate maintained their own livestock for their dinner tables. They were located deep in the interior of the country, far away from decent roads and markets. And there were always a lot of mouths to feed. Tenant farmers supplied fruits and vegetables, bread and cereals, but the meats that found its way to the tables of the estate were often bred, raised and slaughtered on the estates themselves. This ensured freshness, cost effectiveness and a ready and stable supply.

The men worked casually as they stripped the skin off the carcass of the cow. Jackie watched, horrified, as they disemboweled it, casting the offal in a separate tub. The younger man used a chainsaw to remove the cow's head from its body. The angry buzz of the saw reverberated loudly throughout the room. When the head plopped to the floor, he picked it up and teased Jackie with it, nuzzling her face with its nose. Jackie moaned and screamed in terror. The men just laughed.

When the carcass was stripped and gutted, the assistant opened the door to the refrigerated room and the two men pushed and pulled the carcass along the track into the room. She heard them straining as they lifted it from the track and placed it on a hook. They came back out, out of breath, their faces red from the cold. The door slammed shut ominously with a loud bang.

After emptying the large tub of blood into a barrel, the two men sat down to take a rest. Bottles of cold beer emerged and long, overstuffed sandwiches. They sat on small stools and ate silently while they kept their gaze affixed on the frantic ponygirl. Jackie knew that as soon as they were finished with their break the men would attend to her, and she watched with increasing despair as the sandwiches disappeared bite by bite. She found the prospect of being slaughtered and gutted horrifying. To what purpose? Did the men on the estate eat human flesh? Was there some gruesome market for the flesh of young women somewhere? Would she be fed to the dogs, the pigs? Her whole body shuddered at the thought of being eaten.

Jackie realized now that her assumption that she was in safe hands, her pretense that this was some kind of strange dream, that she would be protected from the worse by Jake, was all wrong. She had thought of all of this as some harrowing fantasy that she was not really part of. But the horrible reality was that she was part of it, and now, apparently, past any hope of redemption. She wanted to shout and beg the men for another chance; she would do better, she knew she could. But her pleading eyes were hidden behind the tiny holes in her hood. All the men could see was an anonymous, weaving black head on a brown colored pony, ready for the butcher's knife.

The young man finished his sandwich first. He stood and emptied his bottle of beer and tossed it casually into a rusty, steel barrel near the door. It landed with a loud 'clang!' He stepped to the wall and turned on a long rubber hose, washing away the bloody evidence of the cow's slaughter. He stood behind Jackie and ran the cold water over her sex and her thighs, removing the remnants of her failed bladder control.

The cold water was shocking to Jackie's body and she jumped when it splashed against her skin. She was sure that her butchering was about to commence, but she was wrong. The young man turned off the hose and returned to between Jackie's thighs. He caressed her smooth, brown, proffered rump with his hands and then ran two thick fingers along the gap that separated Jackie's naked, hairless and exposed nether lips. The ponygirl shuddered at the contact. She realized that she was to be subject to one more round of sexual abuse before they murdered her. She clenched her teeth against the thick gag in her mouth, strained against the bonds that held her to the cart and snarled as loudly as she could in protest. But the hand wouldn't go away.

For a man in such a rough trade, he had a tender touch. He lightly traced the outlines of her sex, pushing the nether lips apart gently. He took his time, stroking her, probing carefully, entering only as far as her moistening and dilating pussy would allow. Jackie could feel her passion rising in spite of her anger and hate for the men and what they were going to do to her. She cried out with frustration as she felt the young man's fingers slide deeply inside her, pushing the tender walls of her cunt apart, driving her lusts onwards. A finger teased her engorged clit delicately, causing a tremor of pleasure to run through her body. "No! No! No!" she cried to herself even as her body welcomed the man's expert attentions. It was clear that the men were intent on her suffering one last bout of cruel sexual torment before taking her life. Her pussy was soft and wet with her own secretions when the hand pulled away. There was a moment's pause and she heard the lowering of a zipper. A second or two later, a thick, hard member pushed past the entrance to her womb and buried itself deeply within her. Helpless to forestall her pleasure, Jackie sighed with surrender.

Slowly, deliberately, the young man stroked his cock inside Jackie's moist tunnel. Jackie began to pant with passion. She looked up at the fat man who was still sitting in front of her. He was finishing the last gulp of his beer and as he swallowed it he smiled at her lustfully.

The black headed ponygirl's need was driven higher and higher by the relentless prick. Jackie's rear squirmed and her bound hands writhed behind her as she felt her crises approaching. She decided that she would relish every moment of her orgasm. If this was her last, then make it among the best. Her mind began to welcome her approaching climax. She urged the conscienceless prick on and on. She moaned as she came, her torso jerking and pulling at her bonds. She could feel the man's hot spunk pouring into her as he came as well, his cock throbbing, his hands grasping onto her hips tightly.

When the young butcher's cock left her still pulsing pussy, and her own, intense passion subsided, Jackie began to cry. When he rolled her cart underneath the overhead trolley, Jackie knew that her dismal fate was moments away. She was bent over, the top of her head facing the wall and she could hear chains being run through the pulleys above her. The fat man watched as the younger man attached a chain to each one of her black leather boots. Her boots were released from the floor of her cart and she felt her ankles being pulled up into the air. The chains clattered through the pulley as her feet were bent up above and behind her, causing her back to arch. The young man then released the thick belt around her waist and the inexorable strength of the chains pulled her ankles up higher until her neck was almost twisted back. The collar was then released from the ring in the plank. At the same time, the chains were pulled higher again and Jackie's head swung free from the cart. She was now suspended upside down, her legs splayed widely apart.

When Jackie had felt her legs being affixed to the chains, she lost her fear of calling out and began to beg and plead for mercy. Her muffled cries echoed off of the whitewashed plaster walls of the small room. When she felt her head swing free and realized that she was trussed for the slaughter, her whole body heaved with her sobs. When she sensed the fat man get to his feet, her sobs became a loud piteous wail that emerged even from behind the thick leather plug in her mouth and the shield that covered her lips and chin. She could feel her body swaying as the force of her pleas contorted her torso. Her head was about the level of the fat man's waist and she began to twist and turn her body frantically as he lifted her encapsulated head. Her contortions accelerated as the assistant placed the large, steel tub that had received the cow's blood beneath her in anticipation of the flow her own life's blood into it.

If only the men could see past the accouterments of her bestiality, see her face, acknowledge that she was real, human, Jackie thought desperately. But aside from her unusual dark, chocolate-like skin, she looked like all the other ponies: faceless, featureless, literally devoid of all personality. They would show no more mercy for her than they had for the cow they had just slaughtered. She was just more fun to play with.

Jackie believed that her moment of truth had arrived, but she was wrong again.

The fat man released the strap from behind the ponygirl's head that held in her cruel gag. She was surprised when she felt it pulled from her mouth and grateful for the chance to verbalize her entreaties for mercy. But she just had time for the syllable "pl" to exit her mouth when the man's strong fat hand clamped around her throat, stifling her voice. The assistant handed him something and Jackie felt the object being pressed between her lips. She tried to close her mouth, but the viselike hand that grasped her throat moved to her cheeks and pressed them cruelly. Jackie mouth was forced open and the object was jammed between her teeth, wedging her mouth open farther and farther. When it plopped into place behind her teeth, Jackie realized that he had stuffed a ring gag into her mouth. There was only one purpose for a ring gag.

The fat man released the ponygirl's head and let it swing free. Jackie's collar was built so as to keep her chin uplifted and the ponygirl's enforced vision was of the bloodstained floor beneath her and the empty steel tub into which, shortly, her life's essence would spill. She jammed her eyes closed tightly and wailed. In the meantime, the fat butcher released the ties of his bloody apron from behind him and tossed it to the side. He opened his fly and let his fat, hard dick fall out.

The fat man was in no hurry to complete his work with the ponygirl. He had his lusts to satiate and he wanted to enjoy the pleasant, desirable body of the former human female as long as he could. The man caressed the soft brown skin of Jackie's sides, drawing his hands slowly down her body. Her flesh crawled at the man's touch. These were the hands that would soon draw one of those razor sharp knives across her throat, ending her life. The same hands that would disembowel her, toss her innards aside, peel off her skin. Would they save the tattoo with her name and the crest of the estate? Probably not. She had done nothing noteworthy. In fact, she had failed as a ponygirl. It had been decided that she did not even deserve to live that cruel and lowly existence. Her body held no value for them other than whatever nefarious purpose her lifeless flesh would be put to.

The fat man's hands had reached Jackie's plump and full breasts and he began to massage them lovingly. He squatted down and placed his fat, thick lip on one of her teats and began to lick and suck at it. To her unhappiness, Jackie felt a pull on her loins as the man suckled her, the pleasure of his warm mouth and arduous tongue on her nipple initiating an unwanted spark in her loins. She tried to swing her torso to free herself from him, but he put his hands on her shoulders and held her close. The heavy odor of his sweat overwhelmed her as her face was pressed into his chest. He shifted his mouth to her other breast and teased her stiff, thick nipple with his teeth. Jackie's disobedient body began to respond to his caresses and she moaned through her distended lips expressing both her distress and her passion.

The man rose slowly to his full height, dragging his leathery tongue across Jackie's belly and up to her leaking, splayed sex. When his lips seized her stiff nubbin of pleasure, she moaned again and her widespread legs shook in exquisite protest.

Pausing briefly in his oral ministrations to the captive pony's sex, he took hold of his thick, fat cock and directed it to the hole formed by Jackie's ring gagged mouth. He captured the long, brown ponytail that dangled from the back of her black clad head and used it to impale her mouth on his rampant, hard cock, pressing its fat helmet deeply into her throat. He used the long ponytail to guide her head back and forth on his manhood, forcing her to give it long, slow strokes that left her gasping for air.

Satisfied at his control of the ponygirl's helpless mouth, he resumed his oral attention to her soft, enflamed nether lips and the crevasse between them.

The thick meat rammed home deep into Jackie's throat again and again as the man's tongue drove her lust higher and higher. Caught between terror and pleasure, Jackie groaned and wept in misery and in anticipation of her sexual release. The man leaned his head back and began to flick his tongue over her hardened clit. Jackie moaned, "Ooooooooooommmmm!" as she felt her bodily passion reaching a crescendo. When she came, her thighs shuddered, her body shook. The smell of the man's loins and the salty taste of his cock drove her senses wild as wave after wave of convulsive pleasure ran through her. But the man wasn't finished.

Covering her whole mons with his mouth, delving his thick tongue deep within her hot tunnel, he began to drive the dangling pony to climax again. He had quickened the pace of his manipulation of her mouth on his cock as his own lusts drove him past his dispassionate control. His hips thrust forwards to meet the captive head and the bulging helmet of his relentless cock dragged across the poor pony's defenseless tongue, piercing the entrance to her esophagus again and again. Finally, his cock exploded and the man buried it deeply into Jackie's distended throat. He took her electrified pleasure bud between his lips and suckled at it fiercely, taking the ponygirl over the edge with him. Jackie's body contorted and twisted as the sharp stabs of pleasure pierced her whole being.

As the throbbing of the man's cock began to subside, and the last spurts of his spewm jetted down her throat, Jackie's consciousness returned to her predicament. A wave of misery quickly replaced the physical sensations of ecstasy. She felt the now flaccid cock withdraw from her mouth, and her body swing free of the man's embrace. The satisfied fat man returned his manhood to its lair and zipped up his pants. When Jackie saw him lean over to redon his bloody apron, she realized that her time had come.

The ring gag permitted considerably more communication than her standard gag and Jackie began to plead desperately for her life. "Eeeeeeeeeees! Ooooooooooooo! Eeeeeeeeees!" she called out, her attempt at words frustrated by the contortion of her lips. The fat man's assistant, who had been watching his boss's attack on the ponygirl with intense interest, released the bottom of the black neoprene hood from her collar and then unlocked the collar from behind her neck. It fell free from her head, and dangled from the strap that confined her sweaty, writhing hands behind her. Her smooth, brown neck was now exposed. This precipitated an intensification of the ponygirl's pleas. "Ooooooooooooooo! Eeeeeeeeeeeese! Oooooooooooooooo! Ooooooooooooo!" she cried. She could hear the fat man sharpening his knife, the shrill sound of steel on steel piercing her ears.

Finished with his preparations, the fat man stepped up to his victim. He grasped her ponytail in his hand and pulled her head back, exposing her tender throat. Jackie's mind was racing with remorse and dread. She cursed herself for her greed in accepting Jake's proposal, condemned herself for her halfhearted efforts at pulling the pony cart, begged God for mercy. As the cold, steel blade touched her throat, she closed her eyes and prepared for death.

At that moment, she heard a familiar voice call out. The knife paused, its sharp edge creating a small sliver of parted skin. The voice called out again. The blade was removed and her head was released. The fat man stepped back. Jackie opened her eyes which she had jammed shut in preparation for the piercing pain of the knife. It was her trainer. He was standing a few feet away from her, taking in her splayed, upside down figure. For a moment there was complete silence. Had he come to save her? Or was he here to take one last look at her before she perished? When he finally spoke to the men and signaled them to let her down, Jackie began sobbing with relief.

It took a while for the ponygirl to calm down. They left her lying on the floor of the small room for several minutes as her sobs of relief wore away. When her trainer tapped her on her rump with his riding crop, the ponygirl crawled quickly to her knees. This was a man who held the power of life or death over her. She would do whatever he wanted.

Irkut restored her collar and gag and led her out of the small abattoir. There was a ponygirl cart waiting in the hard packed, dirt courtyard, the same one she had followed there. Irkut connected the brown skinned, hooded pony's nose ring to its back, hopped up onto the seat and, with a flick of the reins, started the journey back to the estate.

Jackie plodded behind the cart mechanically. Her whole body was drained from her terrible ordeal. She didn't know if the whole thing was a ruse or whether her trainer had changed his mind at the last minute. Whatever the case, the message to her was clear. If she wanted to survive, she would have to give over her whole being to her existence as a ponygirl. She could hold nothing back. She would forget

Jake and his promises of money, forget any thought for the future and what might become of her. She had never been so terrified in her life. She could still feel the sensation of the razor sharp blade across her throat. From now on she would obey her trainer as she would a god. For in a sense, he was a god compared to her. She had no right to talk, to think, to do anything without his command or the command of one of the other gods. There was no use fretting over what she had lost, what she had become. She was a ponygirl now and that was that.

By the time that the cart reached the ponygirl barn, Jackie had shaken off the torpor which she had felt when she was first freed from the clutches of the two butchers. When Irkut began to dress her in her racing harness, she felt grateful for the feel of the rough leather against her skin. She stood obediently still as he hitched her to the sulky cart. Although every ounce of her being was supercharged with the need to run, to prove her worthiness, she waited for the flick of the reins before she began her warm up laps around the track, obeying religiously the well known messages sent to her through the straps of leather that led to her bit.

And then she was brought to the starting line. She saw her trainer standing there with his stop watch. She dug her toes deeply into the soft track and coiled her leg muscles, ready to explode into action at her driver's signal. When it came, she pushed off in the dirt with all of her might and pounced into motion.

Running, running, running, that was all she could think of. Her heart pounded and her lungs screamed yet she continued to press forwards as if her life depended on it. Her heavy breasts bobbed madly as she streamed along. She was oblivious to the crack of the driver's whip, insensitive to all distractions as her need propelled her onwards. Her desperate mind commanded her body, "Faster! Faster! Faster!" She would show him, her mind screamed. She was good, she was fast, she was one of the best!

Irkut watched his charge tear along the track with satisfaction. Some ponies had to learn the hard way. He knew that his little charade with the butcher men was cruel, but it brought home an important lesson to the chocolate pony. Running and racing was now her life and if she did not give it her all, then there was no reason for her to exist.

As the straining, heaving pony crossed the finish line, Irkut clicked the stopwatch. He looked down at its face. Six minutes and 58 seconds. Now that was more like it.

CHAPTER THREE
HOW THINGS WORK

Burnham had Jake out on an inspection tour of his growing empire. Jake had assumed the duty of Burnham's personal bodyguard. Kalikastan was a dangerous place and death and murder were usually shrugged off by the authorities, such as they were. Only the members of your particular clan would care, unless, of course, they were the ones who did you in. Burnham wasn't a member of any clan and so he depended heavily on the good graces of the governing council for protection. He had amassed a huge amount of clout there due to the graft associated with the 20 billion dollar gas pipeline that he was building on a 'cost plus' basis for a consortium of Western powers. He was spreading it around liberally and garnishing considerable personal benefits himself.

But to Jake's chagrin, Burnham had turned overall security to a Russian native, Nicholai Borodin. Borodin was a tough motherfucker, and thorough too. His team of black t-shirted guards was all over the estate, alert and conscientious. But this was a double edged sword as far as Jake was concerned. He was sure that Borodin's first loyalty was to his clan and that if for any reason they wanted Burnham, or him, out of the way, that Borodin would act accordingly. And if they were ever going to be able to rescue Maddy and get her out of the country, they would have to do it right under the noses of Borodin's men. Kalikastan was an airtight country and if rumors of their unique women's rights policies surfaced from time to time in the West, proof of them never did. No way would they want a former ponygirl walking around telling her tale. No, Borodin was going to be a problem, Jake was sure of it.

And he was beginning to lose confidence in Burnham's commitment to getting Maddy out too. Burnham had made it clear that he would not authorize any action to snatch Maddy that would undermine his position in Kalikastan. He had moved his corporate brain center here, down to his former secretary, Liz. But, unlike the few top male executives who had been brought over, Liz would never be free to leave. Liz was now one of Burnham's stable of female slaves. He had had her stripped and branded on her arrival and she now wore the tattoo of her new slave name, 'Betty', stenciled across the top of her chest above her deliciously plump breasts. All of the other female slaves had their new slave names tattooed across their chests in two inch high, blue, Cyrillic letters, but Betty's name was in English, an indication of her special status as Burnham's personal body slave and administrative assistant.

Now, it would have been easier if Jake had just reconciled himself to the fact that the attempt to rescue Maddy was over. After all, it was just a job, and if the customer didn't care, then he shouldn't either. But there were several factors that kept Jake in the game, so to speak. First, there was the fact of professional pride. When Jake took a job, he finished it, no matter what it took. He had a reputation to maintain.

Secondly, there was the ethical issue. He had found it necessary to act ruthlessly before in order to successfully fulfill a contract. Men, and women, had died, laws had been broken, things had been blown up. But he had never gone over the edge as far as he had on this job. If he had known how deep it would draw them into the slaving business and for so long, he never would have suggested taking over the operation of the slavers who had kidnapped

Maddy so they could get a foothold with the parties in Kalikastan who had imported her. And once the operation had started, it had to keep going to maintain his and Burnham's bona fides with the bad guys. By now, his people had been responsible for the exportation of more than a hundred young, desirable, luscious American women. He got regular reports from the tall, beautiful blond female version of himself who was running the day to day operations.

Mary Ellen and her gang of lesbian lovelies were about as tough as they came. Somehow they had been able to deal with their qualms over peddling fellow female flesh. The money was good and, if he knew Mary Ellen and her girls, they were probably enjoying the side benefits of being masters over beautiful, naked and helpless young women. He knew firsthand how difficult it was to maintain anything like sexual purity around so much available flesh. But Mary Ellen knew that the slavery operation was short term and that it had to come to an end. She had refused Burnham's invitation to expand operations to the West Coast and Canada. Like Jake, she would do what was necessary, no matter what it was, but no more than that.

But if Jake abandoned the Maddy rescue, he would have done all of this for nothing. He would no longer be able to enjoy the rationalization that he had had a job to do and he did it. All of those innocent young women would have been condemned to lives of abject sexual slavery for nothing.

And then there was the third reason. The third reason was a beautiful, big breasted, young Dutch slave girl named Klara. She had been a gift to him from an estate owner during the time that he was searching for Maddy. Ostensively, he had been looking to buy racing stock for Burnham's new estate, but when he and Irkut visited the various racing estates which had ponygirls for sale, he kept an eye out for Burnham's niece. It was a difficult task since he could never look at any of the ponygirls' faces and had to go by body size and hair color. But he had a photo of Maddy taken before her kidnapping wearing a bikini and he was able to recognize the mole on her left hip. Anyway, the estate owner had taken a shine to Jake and in a moment of generosity gifted him the newly trained Dutch slave girl. There was no way he could say no without insulting the estate owner and so he had taken her with him when he left.

At the time, Jake had just begun to become immersed in the Kalikastani slave girl culture. Owning his own slave girl, being granted the freedom to possess her at his whim, deal with her as he saw fit, literally own her flesh, had been intoxicating. During the months that he had owned her, he had become intensely enamored of her. He couldn't call it love since love implied the recognition of the humanity and personal integrity of the other person. He knew that, as well as he treated her, he still held her in a cruel, involuntary servitude, inconsistent with love. He dreaded the thought of leaving her behind when the job was over. He treated her well, he never beat her, and he envisioned her dismal fate in the hands of another owner with dismay. He didn't know what he would do when the moment of truth came, but he would prolong it as much as he could.

As he rode in the passenger compartment of Burnham's huge motor home, which the billionaire used for long journeys, he imagined the slave girl's supple, pleasing lips caressing his manhood, her big blue eyes staring back up at him in seeming delight. For she did seem to reciprocate his feelings for her. But how could he ever really tell if they were real? Was she in love with him, or merely an obedient, compliant body servant? When she was not free to express disdain or indifference to his demands, could it ever be called love? He had never asked her, but it would have been quite exceptional if she did not intensely detest her sexual bondage, the untold rapes and beating she had received in training, the casual way that the ownership of her body was transferred, or pine for the life she had been torn away from. Life with him was safe and easy as compared to the other fates she could suffer as a slave girl in Kalikastan. Her apparent enjoyment of his caresses and her ardor in caressing him could be mere expressions of gratitude for not treating her as cruel and callously as, by Kalikastani law and custom, he was entitled.

He had left Klara behind at the estate for this trip. He knew that it would be long and he didn't want her all cramped up in one of the slave cages in the van for all that time. Burnham had had the cages built in after he bought it and there were accommodations for four trussed and gagged females. Burnham had filled them up with some recent acquisitions and three of them were crunched up in their tiny cells, gagged and bound, obediently awaiting the pleasures of a master. The fourth, a tiny, blond headed wisp of a girl, was noisily servicing her owner in his large bedroom at the rear of the trailer.

Jake's thoughts turned to the thin French girl that Burnham had acquired about a month ago on a trip to Paris. She was one of the slaves Burnham had brought along for the ride. The billionaire had taken a shine to her when she had waited on his table at one of those fancy restaurants. She was part Vietnamese, and her eyes and skin contained features of both Asian and European races. It was a measure of his growing hubris that he had had her snatched off the streets that evening and brought back with him to Kalikastan.

In Jake's mind, there was no reason for him not to avail himself of her services. Although he knew deep down in his heart that it was wrong, the unfortunate girl had lost the right to determine who took pleasure in her delectable flesh. She had already endured the rigorous torment of slave training in the cellar of Burnham's mansion. Whips and chains had brought home to her her servility. She had been opened and ruthlessly used by the harsh taskmasters of the training facility. Last night, Jake had used the brown haired, English girl who was caged next to her. Today was just her turn.

Rising from his seat, Jake walked down the hallway of the trailer, lurching slightly as it rumbled over the rough roadway. He pulled back the curtain that covered the French girl's steel cage embedded in the wall. The girl looked up at the sudden intrusion of light into her tiny prison. Even with the leather shield gag that covered the lower portion of her face, he could detect her saucy, inviting features, the teasing eyes, the graceful brow that had, unfortunately for her, triggered Burnham's acquisitive instincts. She needed no instruction to crawl out of the small enclosure after Jake had unlocked the door. She rose to her feet obediently as he signaled her to follow him to his room.

Space is at a premium aboard a motor home, even as large a one as this, and Jake's 'bedroom' was small, dominated by a low, double sized mattress. Jake watched appreciatively as the desirable, young female stepped past him and mounted the bed. Her teacup sized, pert breasts rubbed against him as she passed sideways through the small doorway. Once on the bed, she assumed a slave's position, kneeling, her ass resting on her heels, her thighs spread wide. Jake slid the door closed as he stepped into the room.

The girl's large, brown eyes looked at him expectantly. Her hair was black and was cut short in a kind of bob. She was thin, and her collar bones stood out prominently above her chest. Her arms and thighs were delicate and well toned. She had a hard, taut, belly and her naked love lips were thick with a high, pronounced slit between them. She bore the tattooed crest of Burnham's estate on her stomach's flesh, the angry, bare fanged, black hound with fiery, red eyes. Blue Cyrillic letters made an arch over her breasts, recording her new slave name, Natasha.

Jake undressed quickly. His rod had grown hard as he had admired the gracefully moving flesh of the girl, and he approached her on the bed ready for physical passion. His wandering fantasies of Karla's expert oral attentions had stoked his fires. Although his balls ached with need, he had learned to revel in the exploitation of female flesh and he took the time to explore the French girl's body with his small but strong hands and his hungry lips. Sitting next to the kneeling girl, he ran his hands over her smooth, graceful shoulders, down her bound arms and over the outside of her spread thighs. The contact with the French girl's soft, smooth hot flesh enflamed his desire. Leaning over, Jake captured the already hardened, nipple of the girl's left breast with his lips. He ran his tongue over the bumpy areola as he sucked softly on little teat.

One of the principal lessons taught a budding slave girl was the need to respond freely and readily to sexual stimulation. No one wanted to fuck a fish. She was taught to make her body swiftly amenable to physical love at the mere hint of her possible use. In conformity to her training, Natasha had, the moment she had climbed atop the soft, wide mattress, dug deeply into her mind to release her own sexual need. And so, when Jake took possession of her breast, when his hands caressed her naked back, her thighs, her belly, lust swiftly began to bubble to the surface from within her and she gave out from behind her gag a long, wistful moan.

While switching his attentions to the French girl's other firm, passion engorged breast, Jake let his hand trail over the tattooed beast on her belly and dip between her thighs. Her pussy was moist when he found it and he was able to slip his fingers inside her hot channel with ease. The girl sighed again and leaned against him as her need took possession of her. Jake felt her leather encased chin rub against his back as he enjoyed the sensation of her rigid nipple on his tongue. She spread her legs wider to accommodate his probing hand and a waft of her pungent fluids met his nostrils, exciting him, beclouding his mind with passion.

Jake leaned up and removed the thick, leather plug from the girl's mouth. He pressed his lips against hers and drove his tongue deeply within, drinking at the hot moisture of her breath. A groan arose from within his throat as a wave of pleasure flowed through him. The girl kissed him back passionately, her tongue dancing against his, her body pressed against him with need.

But it was not the slave girl's needs that concerned Jake. He had been lingering over the recollection of Klara's skillful attentions to his cock with her dedicated mouth and he wanted the same from the French girl now. He grabbed the ring that was attached to her steel collar and pulled her with him as he leaned back on the headboard of the bed, placing the large, firm pillow behind him. The girl did not have to be told what he wanted, and as he spread his legs in anticipation of her services, she bent over and circled his rampant manhood with her lush, pursed lips.

Jake sighed deeply with pleasure as he felt his cock enwrapped by the girl's ardent mouth. Her hands were still locked behind her, and she had only her lips and tongue with which to excite him. The sight of her upturned bottom, her bound hands writhing behind her, her long, stretched back arched so that her vertebrae formed a bony ridge along it, fueled his lusts, emphasizing the girl's obedient supplications, her surrender to her servility to him.

The girl sucked his cock in long, languorous strokes. Jake placed one limp hand on her brown head as his eyes rolled back and he lost himself in the wet heat on his steely pole. Natasha pressed her face down on him until she had engulfed his thick meat to the hilt, taking the plump, round head into her throat. Moaning softly, as her own lusts were still stoked high, she drew back slowly until the fleshy helmet passed over the edge of her lips. She ran her rough tongue over the underside of the protuberance and, after teasing the cock's tiny opening with the tip of her tongue, pressed her head forward again, pushing the hardened manhood deep within her.

Natasha had learned her oral skills long before she had descended into sexual slavery. Her Algerian boyfriend was a singer in a rock band back in Paris and she had spent many nights partying with him until the early morning night, performing oral adoration of his youthful tool. It was of his firm, vibrant flesh that she thought when she needed to prepare herself for the use of her masters and it was his sleek, swarthy cock that she imagined between her lips now as she made obeisance to Jake's.

When Jake's thighs began to shudder, his breath becoming short, his belly tense, she prepared herself to receive his discharge. Jake gave a loud groan when his cock began to spasm and throb as it spurted his lust's creamy byproduct into the girl's expectant mouth. The girl encouraged his release by long, hard strokes of her mouth, her tongue swirling along the length of the pole, moaning her own desire all the while. The trailer hurtled through the Kalikastani countryside, the rhythms of the road vibrating through its chassis, giving a strange accent to the waves of pleasure that passed through the convulsing groaning bodyguard.

Natasha knew when the man had spent his load. She waited until his cock's throbs had faded to nothingness before she removed her lips from it. She licked the man's member clean as she had been taught and then knelt back, her tiny, firm breasts raised high, her thighs spread wide, ready to receive whatever her master desired to impose or inflict on her next.

It took several moments for Jake to open his eyes as he recovered from his ecstatic release. He saw the brown, doleful eyes of the desirable female watching him expectantly, an expression of deference coupled with apprehension on her face. Her nipples were still taut with need and he could see her glistening, naked, hairless slit between her thighs. He couldn't blame Burnham for wanting her. He wanted her. He could feel the spark of desire rising in his tumescent cock. He wanted to see her face in the throes of passion. He wanted to hear her moan and sigh as her needs overcame her. Rising to his knees, Jake took the French girl by the shoulders and laid her back on the bed. He slid down next to her and delved his hand between her thighs which were slick with perspiration. Covering her mons with his palm, he took her lips and slid his tongue inside her mouth. He could feel her body melt with desire as she sighed and reciprocated his kiss.

Jake teased the girl's wet cunt with his fingers as he used his tongue to enflame the slave girl. When he deftly caressed her hardened bud of passion, she moaned loudly into his mouth and spread her thighs wide apart. Both of their bodies were covered with passion driven sweat and Jake slipped across her torso and imposed himself between her widespread legs. His cock had recovered its stiffness and he guided it slowly into her welcoming passage. As he sank deeply within the sighing, moaning slave girl, he felt her pussy tighten and grasp his manhood.

Natasha climaxed almost immediately when Jake began to stroke his cock along the soft walls of her oozing, tight passage. Jake had taken possession of her head with his hands and watched intently as her climax was recorded on her wildly impassioned face. "Oh! Oh! Oh! Oh!" she cried, each exclamation matching an intensely pleasurable contraction of her canal. Her eyes peered brazenly back at the face of her possessor as she thrust her hips up to match his. As the pulses of pleasure continued, her eyes lost their focus, rolled back into her head and she gave out a loud, long, prolonged moan, "Ahhhhhhhhhhhhhoooooooooh!"

Jake did not pause when the girl's paroxysms of passion relented. His need was on him again and he reveled in the steamy soft insides of the slave girl's engorged hole. His thrusts were long and deliberate as he sought the friction needed to bring on his release. The girl's long, luxurious legs entwined themselves behind his back, drawing him in, her back arched over her bound arms behind her. Each time Jake buried his hot cock deep within her, she exclaimed her pleasure loudly, "Ahhhh! Ahhhh! Ahhhh! Ahhhh!" until her crisis mounted again and her body writhed and shook in orgasm. It was all Jake needed, and his cock exploded, sending jolts of exquisite pleasure through him.

Jake and the slave girl slept side by side on the comfortable bed for the rest of the afternoon. He had diligently affixed the ring in her collar to a chain embedded in the headboard before dozing off. With her arms bound behind her, it was doubtful that she could manage to slide open the door that divided the bedroom from the rest of the trailer, but having care of a slave girl required especial diligence. She was valuable property and if she managed somehow to escape from the van she could be lost. There was virtually no chance that she could escape the country. The disks that dangled from her hairless nether lips proclaimed her as property of the Burnham estate and implied an ample reward for her return. Naked, collared and tattooed females could expect no sympathy from anyone. Female slavery was the lifeblood of the country; anyone assisting an escape would be brutally punished. And if whoever found her decided to keep her or sell her off rather than turn her in to her true owner, she would be no better off than when she had started.

Jake awoke when the van slowed to a stop in the courtyard of Burnham's *pied a terre* in Dlitski, the capital of Kalikastan. It was just dusk and the orange and red flavored light poured in through the window, coloring the small bedroom. He was snuggled up to the French girl with her back towards him and his arm across her hip. The rusty hue of the dying sunlight tinted the young girl's smooth, pale skin. He stroked his hand across her prominent hip and down her thigh. The girl stirred and murmured something as if emerging from a dream. He hoped, for her sake, that it was a good one. Suddenly, her naked body jerked, as if she had been the subject of an electric shock and she twisted quickly away from him. She rolled over to her side, now facing him, and he could see the look of shock and fear on her face. Jake had not restored the girl's gag and she opened her mouth as if to entreaty him. But, she remembered her training, slave girls do not speak unless spoken to, and she bit her lip, grimacing with expectation of punishment.

But Jake had no inclination to add to this poor girl's misery. He sssshed her and stroked her cheek, softening his gaze. The new slave's eyes grew wet as she allowed herself to be calmed by Jake's gesture.

At this there was a heavy knocking at Jake's door.

"Jake!" a deep, loud voice called. "Get your cock out of that whore and get out here! We've got to get ready for the banquet!"

The voice was Burnham's, Jake's overlord, and Jake snorted an affirmative response. He rose and donned his clothes while the black haired slave girl watched him warily. She was beautiful and inviting as she lay sprawled across his bed, her hands still bound behind her. The light from the sinking sun made everything in the room seem softer, more pleasing, and this included the girl's curvaceous form. She had instinctively brought her legs close together to shield her bare beauty lips from view. At a gesture from Jake, she rolled to her back and spread them wide, lifting her knees so that her tender labia parted gently. Slave girls had no right to privacy. The lean, muscular bodyguard was drawn to the girl's deliciously available sex. But he had things to do.

Tonight, Burnham was feting members of the ruling Commission and he was expected to dress to the nines. Burnham was intending to hand out "gratuities" to the Commission members tonight in appreciation of their to date cooperation in his schemes. The pipeline construction had begun and the first of Burnham's whorehouses intended to service the workers had opened. He and Burnham had toured it two days ago, and it was filled with about twenty appealing young women, all bearing the tattoo of Burnham's estate on their bellies. They were, as was Natasha, the first crop from Burnham's slave training facility. They seemed nervous and apprehensive regarding their new responsibilities, feelings that were not assuaged by the harsh tones in which Burnham had given them their final instructions or by the exemplary beating that was administered to one of them. The poor girl had done nothing wrong, but Burnham wanted the girls to understand that slave discipline would be strictly enforced. When the tall, lanky Scottish girl had been freed from the whipping post, her body criss-crossed with red stripes, tears flowing down her unhappy face, she thanked her master and owner by caressing him to completion with her mouth on her knees. Burnham had handled the whip himself. He was becoming quite good at it.

Jake brought himself back to the present and, after tying his shoes, regagged the French girl and unfastened her chain. He led her from his room into the corridor. He was about to reinstall her in her tiny steel prison when Burnham told him to, "Never mind that." The driver, one of Borodin's black shirted security men, smiled as he took hold of the ring in the girl's collar. Jake squeezed past him in the narrow corridor and stepped out of the van. Burnham was waiting for him.

"Let's get inside and get cleaned up. The guests will start arriving in an hour. "

Burnham had taken over a large mansion near the heart of the city. It was set on a four acre park bedecked with late summer flowers and lush greenery. The inside was sumptuous in its appointments, with polished wooden floors and delicately carved maple furniture. The cultured butler led them upstairs. They were followed by two other male servants who brought up their luggage. Burnham took the first room, the master bedroom, and Jake was ushered further down the hall. Like the rest of the mansion, it was finely decorated. It had a large, plush bed. A shapely, red headed slave girl was kneeling in the center of the room in classic slave girl pose. The servant left Jake's suitcase on a stand at the foot of the bed and left.

Jake had no time for the pretty slave and quickly showered and shaved. He donned the tuxedo that Burnham had had made for him, making sure that his Beretta did not leave too noticeable a lump under his left arm. The slave girl had watched him carefully as he had dressed, waiting for some signal for her to perform some duty for him. She was not from Burnham's stock since she bore a different tattoo on her belly, that of a sneering, fierce-eyed fox. Burnham had probably stocked the mansion with local talent either purchased or leased from a nearby whorehouse, Jake thought. Before leaving the bedroom, he admired the girl's long, pillowy breasts and the large, dark areolas that centered on them. The girl's expression was not exactly neutral. Her face had a pleasant expression, almost inviting. She had not moved an inch since Jake came in. Her large, soft eyes met his gaze without shame. Jake promised himself to sample her talents later.

Burnham had really outdone himself, Jake had to admit it. The banquet was an outstanding success. He watched while limousine after limousine pulled up to the mansion and disgorged brilliantly dressed, elegant people, seemingly the cream of Dlitski society. Exquisite appetizers were served in the reception hall to the mansion and dinner was served in a large hall at the rear of the building with vaulted ceilings and bright, sparkling chandeliers. Dozens of slave girls scurried to and fro, mingling with the well dressed and sophisticated men and the elegant, beautiful women who they escorted. It always seemed incongruous to Jake that these women accepted the fact of female slavery so nonchalantly. They barely glanced at the delectable, naked young women who served them, although, from time to time, he saw one or more of the women surreptitiously appraising the graces of a naked, demure slave girl as she delivered a drink or served them a pastried delicacy.

All of the slave girls wore the same heraldic tattoo as the girl in Jake's room. He confirmed the fact that they were leased from an officious looking man who seemed to be overseeing their performance. He was short, well fed, with long, black hair and deep set eyes. His chin was grizzled and interspersed with black and gray whiskers and he looked to be about 45 years old. It was part of Jake's job to assess the guests, always on the lookout for someone who might want to spoil the party, and he picked this fellow out as other than a guest right away in spite of the fact that he was formally attired.

When Jake came up to him he nodded and smiled, his wide lips parting to reveal his large well cared for teeth. "You like the girls?" he asked Jake. His voice was gravelly and deep. He wore on his lapel a pin which was an exact copy of the tattoo on the slave girls' bellies. He obviously had picked Jake out as 'muscle'.

"Of course," Jake answered. "Yours?" he asked even though he knew the answer. He just wanted to keep the fellow talking so as to gain a better assessment of him.

"Yes, yes," the man responded in his sandpaper voice. "From all over, all kinds. A large investment." The man paused. "You are Jake, no? Mr. Burnham's security man?"

Jake nodded his reply.

"There is nothing to worry about. Everybody loves Mr. Burnham. He is a great asset to our country."

"So I'm told," Jake replied.

"Oh, yes, yes," the man insisted. "Some of the girls here tonight are from his services. Pretty American girls." The slave girls exported by Burnham's US operations were received at a central clearing house on the outskirts of the city. From there they were wholesaled out to the various training houses.

Jake looked around. Naked and tattooed, the girls' nationalities were hard to pick out, especially American girls who could be all colors and shades.

"Here, I show you one," the man proffered. He snapped his fingers and got the attention of a shapely, black haired girl who was returning a tray to the kitchen. The girl hurried over and curtsied, her large breasts swaying as she lowered herself and rose. She kept her eyes pointed down at the man's waist. She had a pretty, sharp featured face with heavy black eyebrows. On her bare, lush nether lips hung the disks which denoted her current ownership. The fierce fox tattoo on her belly was evidence of the house where she was trained, in this case the same as her current owner. Four, two inch high, blue tattooed, Cyrillic letters decorated her upper chest, betokening her slave name.

"How may I serve you, master?" she asked in a sweet, pleasant voice. English was the lingua franca for slave girls in Kalikastan since many girls from European countries knew it anyhow. No one wanted them speaking Russian and understanding what was going on around them. So, if they had no English when they were enslaved, they learned what they needed to know fast.

She was wearing black leather bracelets around her wrists and ankles and a shiny, brass collar around her neck. Her feet were bare. When she bent her head to acknowledge her subservience, a lock of her thin, clean, well brushed hair fell across her face. Without thinking, she pushed it back behind her ear, a gesture that emphasized her frailty.

"Where are you from, Dana?" the man inquired. He knew her name from the tattoo across her chest.

"It is not permitted to speak of such things, Master," she answered nervously. She glanced up quickly, anxiously, at the two men who stood before her. Her owner had put her in an awkward position. As her master, she could refuse him nothing. Certain things were beyond contemplation for a slave girl, e.g. refusing an order or speaking out without permission. But slave girls were enjoined from trading personal information with each other or revealing it to anyone else. It happened, but any girl caught telling anyone who she was in her past life, where she came from, was severely punished. All Jake had ever been able to get out of Klara was that she was from Holland.

"What are your duties, slave girl," the man asked her demandingly.

Without looking up, the girl responded in a soft voice, "To serve and obey my masters with all of my heart, body and soul, Master."

The girl didn't have to say where she was from. Her flat, clear English placed her from somewhere in the American Midwest. The man waived her away. With obvious relief, she returned to her duties.

"You see?" the man said to Jake. "American."

Jake nodded. As the girl retreated, Jake had a pang of conscience. He wondered what the girl would be doing now if she hadn't been caught up in the vast web spread out by the slaving operation that he took over for Burnham back in the States. It was early morning there now, a Saturday. She probably would have been just getting up, or perhaps in bed with a young lover, enjoying the warmth of loving flesh, or home with her parents, answering Mom's call to breakfast, getting ready to go out to the mall. What right had he to set in motion the chain of events that brought her here to serve in hell? She didn't look much over nineteen. She had undoubtedly had a bright, full life ahead of her, dreams for her future. But he had to admit that she made a fine slave girl, possessing a fine, round ass and thick, heavy breasts. "Fuck it," he thought to himself, warding off his dangerous self doubts. "I'm going to get a drink."

Jake made his excuses to the slavemaster and wandered off to get a large Bombay gin and ice. There was nothing he could do for this girl. And if he hadn't engineered the takeover of the Jersey slave operation, it would probably still be in business anyway and the girl would probably be just where she was. It had been the only way that he could think of at the time to get into Kalikastan, the only way that he could get a chance to save Maddy. It had to be done. When the Maddy project was over, he would close the slave operation down.

Jake mingled through the noisy, happy crowd. He was not the only security man on duty. Burnham had a few of Borodin's men strung around the room, and the Commission bigwigs had their own men. The security men all watched each other warily. They were easy to pick out though dressed as formally as any of the guests: nervous, cold eyes, nimble hands and a telltale lump under their jackets.

A bell rang signaling the commencement of the main meal. Jake watched as the obedient guests slowly drifted towards the dining hall. Several of the slavemaster's men, all tuxedoed and wearing the fox pin on their lapels, corralled the serving girls and herded them into the kitchen. Jake shot back the remnants of his two ounces of cold gin and followed the crowd of guests.

The banquet room was large and the tables had been arranged in a 'U', with the posts of honor at the top of the 'U' given to the Commission members and their mistresses and/or wives. There were four of them and they carried themselves with the air of people used to wielding great power and instilling timorous respect. The side tables were at least 50' long on each side and had settings for the other forty or so guests. Burnham took a place at the head table next to the current president of the Commission, Oscar Kasparov. He was a large, sophisticated looking man, dressed in a well tailored black tuxedo with shiny silk lapels. If Jake didn't know for a fact that he was a cold hearted gangster, he would have assumed that he was a scion of some European nobility, well acclimated to the things that power and prestige can bring.

The raven haired young girl that sat at his left was one of those things. She had movie star looks, a one in a thousand girl. Her dark eyes were set wide apart, her nose graceful. Her face had that slight lack of symmetry that all true beauties possessed. She was wearing a long, yellow gown that clung to her curves and was held up by thin, white straps. The neckline of the garment was low and loose enough so that when she bent forwards her plump, braless, pale white breasts could be seen, down to the very edge of her light pink areola. Jake had watched as she bent forward from her seat to pluck a sprig of celery from a dish at the top of the wide table. Jake's piercing, hungry gaze met her eyes and she smiled at him, lingering in her pose. She knew what desires she sparked in men, reveled in it, and, undoubtedly, reveled in her inaccessibility. After keeping her eyes locked with Jake's for a long moment, she leaned back and, laughing, spoke to her escort. He nodded knowingly. Jake wondered uneasily why it was that whenever he saw a beautiful woman laughing he thought she was laughing at him.

Jake took a seat high up on the side table to the right of the head table, about four seats down. Burnham sat to the right of Kasparov. Neither one sat actually at the center of the table, which ran between them, solving any disputes as to precedence.

The serving of the many coursed meal commenced almost immediately. The room was filled with gay laughter, the murmur of dozens of amused conversations, the clinking of ice in glasses. A three piece ensemble played mellow folk tunes and the slave girls dashed madly about the tables fulfilling the guests' demands. A brilliant, chilled, sparkling Kalikastani white wine was served, not bad for a native vintage, accompanied by the first course, large, pink and white prawns, flown up from the Persian Gulf, seated in a bed of thick, bright green lettuce. While the guests were chowing down on the delicacy, two men wheeled a large, ten foot wide wooden platform into the middle of the tables, near the opening of the 'U'. Obviously some sort of floor show was planned. The platform had soft, light blue padding over it and large steel rings fastened along its sides. It stood about three feet high and whatever was to take place on it would be clearly visible to all.

The ensemble produced a flourish and the guests all turned attentively to the entrance to the room. The lights were lowered with the exception of a large spotlight that covered the stage in the middle of the tables and a smaller one that lit up the large double doors that led from the large anteroom where the reception had been. Suddenly, the door opened and a tall, hard looking, well muscled man dressed in a long, silken, white robe emerged. He had long, platinum hair that cascaded away from his face and flowed behind him as he walked. He had well chiseled features. His muscular build could be easily discerned from underneath his robe as well as his broad back and thick legs. He strode in purposively, his head held high, a wide grin on his face. Behind him, he towed a long haired, voluptuous, naked, hooded woman. He held a heavy chain in his right hand that connected to a ring in the front of the hood. She had large, heavy set breasts, wide hips, firm, thick thighs. Her hands were locked behind her and she stumbled forwards as the man pulled her into the room. The man stepped quickly to the top of the stage dragging the girl after him, and, pulling the chain high over the girl's head, displayed her delicious charms to the crowd.

The lady and gentleman guests applauded politely at the girl's display. Her long, blond hair was crushed to her neck by the heavy, leather hood that she wore over her head. Thick, leather straps crisscrossed between her breasts and her arms had been tied together and bent up behind her where they were locked onto the straps that bedecked her torso. The pressure from her painfully bent arms caused her twin beauties to present themselves brazenly. Jake looked at her keenly. Like the others, he was used to callously assessing female flesh without compunction for the feelings of the person who might occupy it. There was something strange about the girl that, at first, Jake could not put his finger on. She was standing on her tippy toes and he could hear a stifled squeal from behind the dark brown hood. And then it struck him. The girl had not yet been marked with the symbol of a slave house. The top of her chest, above her breasts, was devoid of dark blue lettering and she still wore the curly evidence of her sexual maturity between her thighs.

Jake realized that the girl was a freshly delivered captive. She had probably been taken directly to Burnham's party from the facility where her long, aluminum shipping tube had been opened. She was almost certainly wholly ignorant of her coming enslavement, where she was, what was to become of her. Like the other beautiful young girls snatched from more than two dozen countries around the world who found themselves ultimately marked and bound awaiting a master's pleasure, this girl had spent many days closely confined, caged and hooded, naked, awaiting her ultimate fate. While awaiting her collection and shipment to Kalikastan, she would have sensed the presence of other captive girls caged around her, heard them whine and plea for freedom, heard the gruff, cruel responses of their captors. Having been kept in darkness, she would not know how long it had been since she had been snatched from her life. She would have no idea where she was now or what was going to happen to her. The sound of the crowd's applause must have been disconcerting.

The man in the middle raised his hand to silence the crowd. He placed his body firmly against the back of the upraised girl and began to stroke and pinch her large, melon sized breasts. The girl's body shook and tremored as a result of the application of the large, strong hands over her pale orbs. Her whine increased in volume and evolved into a low moan when the man took one of her plump tits and squeezed it hard with his mighty right hand. A similar, piteous sound emerged from behind the hood as he tormented her other breast. The crowd, pleased and interested, clapped their hands appreciatively.

The tall, muscular man, still holding the girl's head aloft with his right hand, used his left to unbuckle the straps to the leather hood. When done, he pulled it off with one quick motion. A pair of large, blue, frightened eyes emerged. The girl was wearing a leather shield gag over her mouth and chin, but enough of her face could be seen to suggest her beauty. Her shoulder length blond hair shook wildly as the girl looked around her at the entertained crowd. The man took hold of the girl's neck under her chin with his big, right hand and presented her anguished face for all to see. The girl struggled for her freedom, a fruitless, vain effort given the man's exceedingly greater strength and his obvious experience at handling recalcitrant women. The girl issued another deep moan, louder now due to the removal of the hood. The crowd laughed and clapped hands again at her performance.

The guests around Jake were jesting and joking in Russian, so Jake did not understand what they were saying. But it was clear that they considered the girl's predicament delightfully amusing. The man released the girl's chin, only to circle her torso with his arms and grab her oversized breasts with his strong, meaty hands. He held them tightly, causing the girl to whine, and he lifted her up off of the stage. Her widened eyes reflected her pain and surprise. Her feet swung back and forth beneath her as she sought to regain purchase on the stage surface. When she tried to kick the man who was holding her, there was more laughter and applause from the crowd. The woman next to Jake, a pretty, young, lanky redhead, could hardly contain herself. She flashed her wildly amused eyes at Jake and clapped her hands loudly. She called out something to the man on the stage and the other guests all around laughed harder.

Jake could not find amusement in the girl's predicament. He had come to view female slavery as a fact of life, but abhorred unnecessary cruelty. He looked over at Burnham. The billionaire was watching the reactions of the crowd carefully. His face carried proof of his happiness that the entertainment was proving to be a hit. He leaned over to Kasparov and spoke to him. Kasparov smiled broadly and clapped him on the back. The delectable black haired beauty to Kasparov's left was gazing intently at the spectacle. Jake thought he detected a note of horror in her visage.

The man on the stage slowly brought the girl back down to her feet. When she had regained her balance, he placed one of his arms around her neck and wrapped his feet around her legs, imprisoning them, and then forced them spread widely. His other hand ran lightly over her firm belly and slowly worked its way down to her faint, but visible, blond bush. He caressed the gap between her legs lightly and then stroked the inside of her thighs. The girl protested his attention to her intimate place loudly through her gag. Her breasts swayed and shook as she struggled. The man placed his hand between her legs and clamped his fingers tightly over the girl's fur covered nether lips, squeezing them harshly while, at the same time, jamming his arm against the girl's neck. The girl whined and moaned at the pain. Her eyes clenched shut and her brow wrinkled. Her cheeks were wet with her tears. Jake saw the man whisper something in the poor girl's ear and she seemed to nod some form of assent. When he released his grip on her mons, her body relaxed and her struggles ceased.

Having achieved the girl's reluctant cooperation, the man began a slow, steady, sensual assault on her body. The crowd grew hushed as he stroked her breasts gently, pinching the large, fat nipples. His soft, mooning voice could be heard faintly, as he urged the girl into a passionate response. His hand fell down her stomach back to her sex. His large hand covered it and began to rub it almost tenderly. The girl must have felt the nascent emergence of her lust, because her body shuddered and she resumed a feeble resistance. The man responded by clasping her neck tighter with his huge, muscular left arm, just enough to remind her of the consequences of rebellion. Jake watched intently, his qualms dissipated by his lustful responses, as the man opened his right hand and drew a thick finger the length of the girl's slit. He traversed its length several times and was finally rewarded with its lubrication. Slowly, he insinuated his fingers deeply into her canal, spreading the hairy lips. When he spread her moisture to her pleasure bud, the girl's eyes rolled back and her body seemed to sag.

Now that the man had excited the girl's lusts against her will, he began to playfully tease her. He stroked her cunt slowly and expertly and then withdrew to caress her soft, inner thighs, her flat, hard belly, and her blood engorged breasts. Slowly, but surely, the young woman's body began to react to his deft caresses. Jake could see the girl's breaths become deeper as her lusts were driven onwards in spite of her. Her pelvis involuntarily thrust out to greet the hand when it returned to her loins, and she moaned a moan of pleasure when the man buried two thick fingers within her.

The brightly illuminated couple stood out in the otherwise darkened room. When the man began to intensify his attentions to her flooded channel, the girl's moans became more marked. Something must have brought the girl's consciousness back to where she was and what was happening to her, since her eyes opened with a start. Her eyes darted around the room, the audience obscured by the spotlight shining in her face, but the outlines and shadows of the amused people still visible. Perhaps it was the shock of her impending sexual climax that made her return to consciousness regarding her predicament, for shortly thereafter her body began to rock and sway in the man's arms. Her motions were recorded by her large, swaying breasts. Her hard, thick nipples stood out amidst her large, dark areola. The man began to flick his finger at the point of pleasure at the apex of her cunt and her eyes closed again. She screamed a moan of protest and passion into her gag as her body began to convulse and squirm. "Mmmmmmmmmmm! Mmmmmmmmmmmmm!" she cried out. The man's hand drove her on and on. When she gave out another long, agonized moan, the audience broke its mesmerized silence and began to applaud wildly. Her creamy thighs shuddered, her breasts shook. "Oooooomph! Ooooooomph! Ooooooooomph!" she screamed as her orgasm overcame her. Finally, the girl's body went limp and the man raised his sticky fingers in the air triumphantly. He received a standing ovation.

This was the signal for the house lights to go up and the meal to continue. While salad was being served by the coterie of naked slave girls, the man doffed his white, silk robe. There was a chorus of appreciative oooos and ahhhhhs at his splendid, muscular physique and his long, thick, rampant manhood. The houselights were still dimmer than the spotlight that brightened the man and woman on the stage and the man continued the show by letting the girl slip to the floor of the stage, spreading her legs and mounting her.

All through dinner, the man continued his sexual assault on the girl. He received smatterings of applause each time he manipulated the girl into a different contorted position and reinserted his steely manhood deep within her. The leather shield over her mouth and chin was removed to reveal a large ring gag that spread her teeth apart widely. Grabbing the girl by the hair, he forced his cock through the opening and proceeded to give her a vigorous throat fuck. The girl sputtered and gagged and protested while her mouth was raped for the very first time. She was on her back on the floor of the stage, her head tilted back to render the wide circle formed by her distended lips convenient for the man's thrusts. His knees were on either side of her head and he faced her feet. Her legs were spread and tied off at the ankles to rings in the side of the stage, and she yanked at her confinements desperately, frantic to dislodge the thick meat that had invaded her throat. The man's body was covered with a sheen of sweat and his well developed muscles rippled every time he moved. The girl seemed puny and helpless beneath him, as surely she was. By the time that the remnants of the main course was removed, Jake counted at least three more orgasms for the pitiable girl and two for the man. The wine had been changed to a hearty, fruity local approximation of a Zinfandel. Jake savored the dregs of his glass as the man finally pulled his thick, hard weapon from the exhausted girl.

While the dishes were cleared and bowls of fruit and nuts distributed, the two men who had rolled out the stage brought a set of long, shiny steel pipes out. It took them a few minutes, but when they were done, the pipes had been assembled into the form of a gibbet above the stage. The girl had taken no notice, her sweaty, limp body lying in a heap. When the two men left, the male performer, his thick, limp cock swaying between his muscular legs, grabbed the girl by her long, blond hair and pulled her to her feet.

The girl screeched with pain as her hair was rudely yanked. The ring gag was still in her mouth and the sounds of her cries were distorted by her mouth's round configuration. The man cuffed her face and slapped her twice across her heavy, pale breasts. The girl, tears flowing down her face, and, uttering obscure unintelligible imprecations, nodded earnestly at the man while cringing in anticipation of more blows. She stood there docilely, her eyes sorrowfully taking in the merriment going on around her, her face etched in unbelieving wonder. She had surely never imagined that a world like this existed, never mind that she would ever be the principal prop in an explicit display of male sexual power. Undoubtedly, she had heard the applause and cheers as she was tormented. Her mind would be hoping that this was all part of some evil dream.

The male performer loosened the girl's arms from behind her back. Jake watched the wave of pain pass through the girl as blood renewed its circulation to her freed limbs. The man quickly brought her hands around in front of her and applied a set of thick, leather bracelets. He locked them together, binding her wrists. The gibbet like structure extended over the center of the stage and a chain dangled from the edge of its extended arm. The chain's other end passed through rings along the top of the horizontal pole and down the vertical pole that was set in the floor of the stage. The male performer reached up and grabbed the chain and hooked it to the girl's bound wrists. Her body swayed and she looked around warily as the man stepped back to the vertical pole and found the other end of the chain. When he pulled on it, the girl's arms began to rise. The girl had been in a kind of a daze, but the upward pressure on her wrists startled her into wakefulness. Frightened, she turned to look at her tormentor, who was standing behind her. At the same time, the man continued to pull on the chain that led to her wrists until the girl was standing on her tippy toes.

The slave girls had just finished pouring cups of aromatic coffee for the guests and distributing little silver bowls of rich vanilla ice cream. The man on the stage finished his adjustments to the girl's status by applying thin leather straps around her ankles and thighs, binding them together tightly. The abject, young female's face was distorted by fear and apprehension. Maybe she had seen a fellow kidnap victim worked over by a lash when she had arrived at the slave clearing house before she was brought here. Maybe it was just instinct. But she seemed to know that she had been trussed and secured for some nefarious reason. Her large, blue eyes pleaded to no one in particular for mercy. Her body swayed and jerked as she frantically tested her securements.

When she saw the man present a short, tasseled whip to the audience and receive in response their excited applause, she began to twist and turn in her bonds frantically. She called out, 'Oooooooouuu! Oooooouuuuu!" through her gag in vain protest. The thick, round gag of reinforced leather that distended her mouth prevented the formation of any words. It was not clear whether she was speaking in English or some other tongue. But the import of her exclamations was crystal clear. Their sound provided added delight to the callous audience.

The man bowed to the head table and Kasparov, as the main guest, gave the signal for the man to proceed. He turned to the dangling girl, drew his right arm fully behind him and brought the fearsome instrument forward. The whip landed across the girl's midsection. Her body stiffened as she shrieked in pain. Her eyes shot open widely and her head jerked back. The sounds of her piteous complaints resounded through the room. All eyes were on the spectacle. Even the slave girls, who had posed themselves along the walls of the room behind the diners, watched with steely intensity. They had all experienced the whip at one time or another, some of them many times. They knew what the girl was feeling now. No way did any of them want to take her place.

The naked, male performer worked his way all over the front of the poor girl's body with the whip. Bright red stripes appeared wherever the whip landed. The girl's body writhed and her large breasts swung wildly, as the methodical torment continued. She cried and screamed in futile protest. When her breasts were whipped, the girl's cries seemed to reach a new crescendo. Her face was contorted with fear and agony. When the man went behind her, she let out a long, loud pitiable wail. There was just enough room to swing the whip, and the helpless girl's torment continued as the man lathered her back, her pale rear globes and the back of her graceful, thighs with the whip.

Jake was hypnotized by the vicious tableau in front of him. He had seen girls whipped many times, ponygirls too. He was always shocked afterwards at the fierce sexual need that gripped him when he did. He was not alone, of course, and the crowd of guests were transfixed by the girl's agony. Suddenly Jake felt a long, thin hand caress his right thigh. The lanky, redheaded young woman sitting next to him, apparently overwhelmed by what she was witnessing, pushed her hand between his legs under the table until she had hold of his thick, hardened cock through his dress pants. He looked to his right. The beautiful young girl's eyes were firmly affixed in front of her, not registering her capture of his joint. Jake moaned quietly as she rubbed and squeezed it. Lustfully, he spread his thighs to accommodate her while his hands grasped the edge of the table. He felt himself building to a climax, driven by the scene of the suffering girl on the stage and the manipulation of his tool.

All of him wanted the intense, exquisitely pleasurable release he knew he would find. But, rationality struggled through the haze of lust and finally won out. He didn't want to have to walk around for the rest of the night with a tell tale stain on his pants. He quickly placed his hand under the table and grabbed the girl's wrist, removing her hand from his cock. The girl looked at him. She had an animalistic sheen of passion on her face. She licked her plump, luscious lips luxuriously, invitingly. Clasping his hand tightly, she returned her attention to the torture of the blond haired slave girl to be.

All around the crowd demonstrated the overtaxing of their libidos. Men and women were kissing and groping each other. A few had slave girls on their laps, their hands buried in their quims. And across the way, Jake could see the bottom sides of naked, feminine feet poking out from under the tablecloth denoting the fact that a slave girl was paying oral attention to a guest's needs.

Finally, the whipping stopped. The blond headed girl dangled limply in her bonds, moaning her dismay at her treatment. Bright, angry red lines covered her body. The man's huge digit was hard and he stroked it wantonly as he nodded and bowed to the pleased guests. The lights came up again and slave girls scurried to remove the guests' desserts and pour more coffee. Two slave girls pushed carts down behind the line of guests. The carts were loaded with two dozen different bottles of brandies and aperitifs. The slave pushing the cart on Jake's side was the American slave girl, Dana. If Jake had had previously any doubts that he would violate her body if given the chance, he had lost them. Admiring frankly her luscious form, he asked her for three fingers of Remy Martin and, as she leaned over to place the snifter on the table before him, he took the opportunity to caress the inside of her thigh. The skin was soft and smooth, as he knew it would be. The girl paused to let him have his way with her. He moved his hand up to her hairless slit and pinched the two love lips together softly. The girl looked down at him and smiled, a forced smile, a dutiful smile. This was a girl not yet fully acclimated to her new life. Her pretty breasts shuddered slightly as she spread her legs obediently. It was only when he felt the release of her moisture below and was able to slide his finger easily down the length of her hairless slit that Jake released her. He brought his hand to his nose, drawing in the girl's musky scent and wondered if she would be available later.

The torment of the blond haired girl was not over. The two assistants removed the steel gibbet from the stage. The male performer had released the girl and she fell to her knees. She bent over, her head to the floor, sobbing. The men returned with some more equipment. A pole, about three feet high, was affixed to the floor in the front of the stage. A stanchion just a little taller was placed about three feet away from it. When the equipment was in place, the male performer leaned over and grabbed the girl's lush, blond hair and again pulled her to her feet. She moaned and cried as she was lifted. Her whole body bore evidence of her whipping, angry red stripes crisscrossing like a thatch upon her. She looked as disconsolate and unhappy as a woman could be. The man guided her over to the stanchion. She had to proceed with little hippity hops because her ankles and thighs were still bound by the leather belts the man had placed there before her whipping. Her breasts shook and danced invitingly on her chest with each little jump. There was dismay in her eyes as she considered fearfully what torture or degradation was now in store for her.

The stanchion was firmly embedded in the stage and the man hooked the belt around the girl's ankles to its base. He crossed in front of her and unfastened her wrists. When the girl saw his stiff, engorged and ready cock, she cringed and gave another loud sob. She knew that her ordeal was not over. As he fastened her wrists behind her back, she looked out at the crowd piteously. Seeing only callous, lustful faces, she closed her eyes and resigned herself to her fate.

The male performer came back from behind the girl. He had a leather collar and he clasped it around her neck, lifting her now tangled and knotted hair away from her neck first. He pulled on a ring on the front of the collar, forcing the girl to bend over. Her head came level with the top of the steel pole in front of her. The man clipped the ring to a hook on the top of the pole.

The naked, distraught girl was now bent over forward, available once more for sexual abuse. Her face was turned up towards the leering faces at the head table. The man turned and smiled to the crowd on both sides of him, holding his thick dick in his hand. A series of applause and catcalls accompanied his traverse so that all of the audience could appreciate the girth and length of his manhood. He returned his gaze to the head table, bowed and turned back to the girl. Her head was just below waist high, and the ring gag gave the man ready access to her mouth. Holding her head steady with his fist in her hair, he slowly plunged his manhood into the proffered hole until it was buried to its hilt.

The voluptuous blond girl choked, sputtered and moaned as the thick cock pierced her throat for the second time this night. The man stroked his cock in her mouth slowly and deliberately, pausing occasionally to let the girl take deep, anguished breaths. Her breasts flopped back and forth beneath her and her legs strained at their bindings. Her bound hands writhed and pulled at their confinement. For several minutes, the man pleasured himself in the girl's throat. She accepted it noisily, tearfully crying "Gaaaaaaaa!" each time he buried its head deep within her. But the man's exploration of the girl's mouth and throat was merely a preliminary. When he finally pulled it from her gaping oral cavity, it was wet and slimy. He patted the girl appreciatively on the cheek and then proceeded to take up a position behind her. With her pussy's lips tightly squeezed between her thighs, there was only one available target for the man's lust.

The man's large hands spread the girl's rear cheeks and he placed the end of his cock in place to pierce her anal ring. When the girl felt the man's cock press at the entrance to her tiny, wrinkled brown star, she stiffened. When he pressed it slowly forward, she began to frantically beg and plead. Her sounds made no sense as no words could be formed by her mouth. But a loud, garbled approximation of language flowed from her all the same. "Arrrrrrrghhhh! Unctsaaaaay! Oooooooh! Achhhhhhhh!" she screamed. The pain of the stretching of her anal tissues to accommodate the man's huge prick was clearly evident as her body shuddered and shook. As he mercilessly continued his harsh invasion of the narrow ring of flesh, she waved her head back and forth and screamed, causing her large, rotund breasts to sway beneath her. Slowly but surely, the man sank deep within her bowels. The girl's screams turned to moans. The worst, the stretching and tearing of the delicate ring of flesh that surrounded her anal opening, was over. Although the man's large cock had been covered with her slick saliva to ease his penetration, the man's size would have split any woman's rear entrance.

His cock nestled deep inside the unfortunate young woman, the male circled his hands underneath her torso and took hold of her beauteous breasts. Using them as an anchor, he began to saw his steel hard cock back and forth. The man's large, muscular body covered hers almost completely. Each time he drove his cock home, the girl gave out an exclamation of dismay. Tears were flowing freely down her face. Soon the girl would learn to derive pleasure from the use of her small, tighter entrance. But for now there was only shame and pain. Both of the performers' bodies were covered with sweat and the strong spotlight made their skin shine. The man's hands crushed the girl's breasts and he cruelly pinched and twisted her thick, hard nipples while she writhed and struggled beneath him. It took several minutes, but suddenly the man's head rolled back, his lips spread in a wide, lecherous grin. His thrusting became harder, drawing louder and more desperate moans from the girl. And then he called out, "Arrrrrrrgh! Arrrrrrrrrrrgh! Arrrrrrrrrrrrrrrrgh!" as he pumped his semen into her depths. He grasped the girl's bulky breasts tightly as his whole body tensed. His orgasm was intense and prolonged. The girl blubbered and sobbed in dismay.

And then it was over. His thrusting slowed, his grasp of the girl's tortured globes relaxed. He pulled his now limp manhood from her ass. An assistant handed him a small towel and he wiped his detumescent equipment clean. Another handed him his robe. He donned it while the assistants attended to the limp, passive female. Her shield gag was reinserted in her mouth and the hood tied back over her head. Her neck was released and she was brought back to a standing position. When her ankles and legs were unbound and the hook to the base of the stanchion released, the man took hold of the ring on her hood and pulled her to the front of the stage. He bowed low to the audience, forcing the girl to join him in exhibiting appreciation for the crowd's enjoyment of her torment. The men and women clapped and yelled at the pair, standing in their places.

Even Burnham and Kasparov were on their feet. In fact, the only exception to the display of gratitude for the enthralling performance in the room seemed to be the black haired, model class beauty that was Kasparov's companion. Her face was ashen and she clasped her hands tightly together. Jake watched her face as the effect of the cruelty she had witnessed sank into her. She was apparently not a native to Kalikastan. "Did she think all of this female slavery was fun and games?" Jake thought. Kasparov glanced at her for a second, but ignored her discomfiture.

The applause lasted a full two minutes. Finally, the man cut it short by waving his hand at the crowd. He affixed a chain to the blond girl's hood and guided her carefully down the stairs at the back of the stage. Towing her, he walked briskly from the room, the unhappy female stumbling blindly behind him.

Burnham took up a spoon from the table and clinked it repeatedly against a glass until the guests silenced themselves. He motioned for them all to sit.

"Ladies and gentlemen," he bellowed in his deep, authoritative voice, "I hope that you have appreciated tonight's entertainment and dining experience. While I am new to Kalikastan, I have quickly grown to love the country and its people." He paused here. "And of course, its special cultural attractions." The audience laughed.

"I want to thank the members of the National Commission for their faith in me in granting me Kalikastani citizenship. As a measure of my appreciation, I have prepared tokens of gratitude." Burnham waived to the back of the room. Four of Borodin's security men advanced to the head table. Behind each, their collars connected to a leash, were the four slave girls that Burnham had brought down with him from the estate, naked and refreshed. The French girl, now named Natasha, was among them and her eyes frantically took in the strange scene of the happy guests, the busy, naked slave girls and the plethora of sunglassed, harsh visaged security guards that lined the walls. All of the four girls bore on their bellies the distinctive fierce-looking canine tattoo signifying their training at Burnham's estate. Each carried in her hands, which were bound before them just under their enticingly beautiful, nude breasts, a finely wrapped package, topped by gold and silver bows. The slave girls were brought around the back of the head table and their leashes were handed off to each of the four smiling and happy Commissioners. When the transfer was complete, the slave girls curtsied and presented the packages to their new owners. Fear and apprehension as to their new fates was etched across the politely smiling face of each deferential slave girl. Memories of his fine afternoon with the French girl swept through Jake's mind. Well, there would be no more of them. He was happy that he had sampled her pulchritude when he had the chance.

The packages contained the first of the many payouts they were to receive under the agreement that brought Burnham and Jake entrée to the country. Kasparov's was, of course, the largest as suited the President of the Commission. Jake saw the French girl, Natasha, nervously hand over her package to the crime lord. Kasparov placed it on the table in front of him and grabbed the girl's bound hands and raised them over her head with one hand. He pulled her closer to the table so that the audience could get a better look at her while his other hand tested and caressed her pretty, pert breasts. The other Commissioners did the same.

Kasparov turned to look at Burnham, pleased at his new toy. Having some of his trained slave girls in the households of the Commissioners was a good advertisement for Burnham's new slave girl training operation. Everyone would want one now. So it was a gift that benefited both parties. But the cash was without strings. Watching the well dressed, almost regal Commissioners gracefully receive Burnham's largess, the audience clapped enthusiastically, for they knew that the largess contained in the packages would find its way trickling down to them.

"I am a man of action and not words," Burnham continued. "So I will not bore you with a long speech." He lifted his glass. "To Kalikastan, to the National Commission and especially to Oscar Kasparov!" The guests raised their glasses and cheered. Jake shot back the rest of his Remy. He looked around for the brandy cart.

Kasparov rose and hugged Burnham tightly. There were more cheers and shouts in Russian. Kasparov waived the crowd silent.

"Friends," he called out to them, he was speaking in English so that Burnham could understand him. "We have long desired a friend of Mr. Burnham's power and prestige. He has earned the everlasting friendship of the Commission and all citizens of our country. I accept his gracious gifts. But what kind of man would I be if I did not have one for him, eh?"

Kasparov was smiling at the crowd. They shouted and laughed back at him. "And so I have brought one with me tonight." He looked over to the beautiful black haired woman who had sat uncomfortably beside him all night. He motioned for her to rise. She looked back at him warily and, afraid to show him any disrespect in front of the unruly crowd, she rose tentatively from her chair. The girl was obviously not a native of the country. What she heard from Kasparov's mouth would barely register with her. What had she to do with a gift for the American billionaire? What was going on here? Was all of this really real?

"Let me introduce to you my special guest, Katya," Kasparov continued. He guided her to the center of the head table with his outreached hand. She took it nervously, a simulacrum of a smile on her face. Suddenly, it seemed to dawn on her what was up. She began to try and remove her hand from Kasparov's grasp. He held it tightly. Jake saw two of Kasparov's security men step forward. They had stood silently behind their lord and master throughout the night keeping a wary eye on the guests and on Jake. Jake reached nervously into his jacket and placed his hand on the grip of his Beretta, watching for any sign that the men intended his boss any harm. He saw Kasparov take Katya's hand and placed it in Burnham's.

"My gift to you, my friend, the most beautiful girl in all of Croatia," Kasparov intoned with a sweeping gesture of his hand.

Katya's nervousness visibly increased. Burnham brought her hand to his lips and kissed it. He looked up at his fellow slavemaster. "I thank you, my friend," he said looking at the gangster. He looked back at the beautiful young woman hungrily. "Welcome to Kalikastan," he said to her, a sharp, cold edge to his voice. As Katya's face began to register a protest, Kasparov's men sprung into action. One of them took hold of her arms and pulled them behind her back. The girl's eyes widened and she opened her comely, desirable lips in protest. The other man deftly slipped a thick, leather gag into the girl's mouth. He had it buckled behind her head in a trice. Meanwhile, the first man had pulled a black cotton hood from his jacket pocket. He pulled it over her head and drew the string at its base tight, sealing it around her pretty neck. The girl struggled frantically, but the second man held her by the upper arms, lifting her from the floor. She waved her black hooded head and tried to kick out, but the first man caught her leg and applied a steel bracelet around her ankle. It was connected by a small, foot long steel chain to another bracelet. He pulled her leg down and attached the other bracelet to her dormant ankle.

Jake could hear the astonished and terrified young woman squeal and protest from behind her gag. A sharp jab to her stomach quieted her immediately and her body went limp in the security men's arms.

Kasparov addressed the American billionaire. "May I?" he asked.

Burnham nodded at him and said, "Be my guest."

Kasparov stepped up to the slumping, hooded girl. He took the bodice of her slinky yellow dress in both hands and ripped it asunder. The girl's well formed, grapefruit sized breasts sprung free. Kasparov pulled her forwards to present her to the crowd. He received a resounding round of applause. A chain was attached to the bottom of the girl's hood and the free end handed to Burnham. He smiled while he examined her naked flesh appreciatively. She was wearing a tiny yellow thong and Kasparov's men quickly had it removed using sharp switchblade knives. Her black bush was neatly trimmed and sat between slender, well formed, smooth thighs. Burnham ran his hand over her barely disguised nether lips. The girl was stirring now, having recovered some of her loss of breath from the blow to her stomach. She tried to arch her loins away from the probing hand, but the men who held her forced her compliance with Burnham's rude examination. After a moment, the billionaire tore himself away from his pretty, new possession. Addressing his guests he said, "And now it is time to say good night. If you look under your plates, you will see attached the name of one of our lovely servers. You may take her home with you tonight as my favor to you. But," he added, pausing briefly, "you may have her only for tonight. A car will be by to collect her in the morning. My caterer would be out of business if you deprived him of his workforce."

Another round of applause and laughter followed and the guests started to scramble about the room to locate their playthings for the evening. The slave girls were dutifully lined up at the exit to the ballroom, their arms bound behind them, chains with leather handles on the ends dangling from their steel collars. To the sound of delighted laughter, one by one, the pretty, naked, young slaves were collected by the guests and led from the room.

Jake had released his hand from his pistol. He flipped over his dessert plate to find the name 'Dana' taped to its bottom. He looked up and saw the caterer smiling at him knowingly. Jake smiled back, pleased.

CHAPTER FOUR
WHAT A SLAVE GIRL KNOWS

Klara strolled quickly across the well manicured, grassy field that separated the carriage house from the Burnham mansion. She was carrying back a large tin tray on which sat the remains of the dinner for Jake's crew who lived there, Martinez, Curley, Tucker and Leon. The men had had a raucous meal, downing several pitchers of the strong, dark, local ale and playing with the more than compliant slave girls who had been assigned to them for the day. Jake's men were a class apart from the other men at the estate in the eyes of the slave girls. Not born and bred to cruelty, their demands were usually within the bounds of civilized normality and their love making gracious and appreciative. There were no whips in the carriage house.

Of the four men, only Tucker had become enamored of the sport of pony girls. While the other men spent their days mostly fucking and drinking, he hung around the pony barn helping tend the numerous ponies that Burnham had accumulated. He would help with the ponies' morning ablutions, cleaning them, feeding them and giving them their morning sexual workouts. It was a well known tenet of the care and maintenance of pony girls that they needed to be given a regular, heavy diet of sexual stimulation and satisfaction. And so each morning, Tucker would bury his face between the wide spread thighs of one or another black hooded pony girl, bringing her to exquisite satisfaction. Or, if in the mood, he would satisfy himself in their hairless loins, giving them a slow, masterful fuck until they shook and mewed with pleasure. On some days, he would stroke them to satisfaction with his hand, enjoying the sight of their bodies exhibiting their growing lust, the swaying of their pretty breasts as their chests heaved, the trembling of their strong, pale thighs as they came.

Tucker had also taken on the specific responsibility for the care of Burnham's work ponies, Dora and Flora. Burnham had obtained them off of the secondary pony market, their usefulness as racing ponies being spent. Seven years of racing had taken the edge off of their abilities, and they were no longer considered competitive, especially with younger, stronger ponies being developed every year. Burnham liked to take them out for a spin every afternoon when he was in residence, wheeling them around the narrow roads and trails that surrounded the estate. When Burnham was away or too busy to give them their daily exercise, Tucker would hitch up the two heavy set, shapely, blond ponies and take them for a run himself. The ponies were often used by the estate hands to move work materials and supplies around the estate pulling a small wagon. But it was Tucker that put them to bed every night. And woe betide the man who abused them needlessly.

While Jake was away, Klara was left in the care of his otherwise idle men. Jake had wanted to take Curley and Martinez with him on Burnham's trip, but the boss had nixed it. Jake was worried that their idleness would take their edge off. They were all hard men, capable of quick and ruthless violence when necessary. But they were heavily outnumbered by Borodin's security men. Jake hoped that when the time came, if it came, the men would be still capable of making a good account of themselves in any showdown. Time would tell.

Klara had spent the most of the day in the carriage house, like she did almost every day since Jake had brought her here. She had been terrorized when she found herself suddenly and casually gifted to him several months ago. He seemed fierce and cruel to her. But from the very first night that she spent with him, he had treated her tenderly and with care. It was a world apart from the brutal and callous treatment she had received while being broken to her slavery. Since then, she had become bound to him in every sense of the word. When she thought of him, she could almost forget that she was living a surreal existence as his sexual property. She genuinely enjoyed giving the man pleasure. She had learned to use her now skilled lips and tongue to tease his manhood for twenty or thirty minutes before accepting his creamy, hot discharge as he groaned and grunted in ecstasy. When he filled her steamy tunnel with his hard, thick cock, she lost herself in her passion. She had learned to love the long, slow strokes he would administer to her when he fucked her ass. When he was 'home', she always slept with him, even when he had brought one of the other slave girls into his bed. She knew it was shameful, but she thrilled to see him take his pleasure with the other girls. He was truly her master and she was his slave.

The conversion from a 21 year old divinity student in Amsterdam to a servile slut had been a difficult one for Klara. Her father was a Calvinist minister in a small village in the north of the country and she had lived a somewhat cloistered existence. He had quailed at the thought of her going off to the evil, dark city of Amsterdam for advanced schooling, but she had convinced him that she would be all right. He had arranged for her to stay with a devout family on the outskirts of the city and she was carefully monitored.

Even so, Klara, or Renate, as had been her preslavery name, had developed a romance with a boy from Rotterdam. He was also studying to be a minister and they envisioned a life together doing God's work. Pieter was devout and righteous and had forsworn premarital sex. Renate had made the mistake of letting a boy go too far in high school, but just once, and the memories of that experience were not good. The boy had broken her hymen with one hard thrust and had emptied himself inside her almost immediately. Based on this experience, she was content to wait to consummate their passions for each other as Pieter insisted, but there were two problems. They kissed and cuddled on occasion as young couples are want to do, and Renate often left Pieter's company with a deep, physical desire for completion. Her breasts would ache with the evidence of her aroused lust and she would have to pray to stop from giving herself relief in her tiny bed in the attic of the house in which she was staying. She cursed herself for her lustful, sinful nature, but often dreamt of Pieter's passionate embrace and his rock hard prick, which she had had the temerity to touch only once.

The other problem had been how to explain to Pieter the fact that she was no longer a virgin. She sometimes cried at night in fear that when Pieter found out that she wasn't pure, he would desert her. She tried many times to tell him, but never had.

But father had been right. One night, after studying late for exams, Renate had been standing on a well lit corner within the university campus waiting for a bus. She did not take much notice of the two young men, ostensively students, who were standing behind her. A black van pulled slowly down the block and stopped at the red light. Just as the yellow light came on for the other direction, the van door slid noisily open and Renate felt herself propelled forcibly towards it, the hands of the two 'students' behind her gripping her arms tightly. Her books and carry bag spilled to the ground. She didn't even have time to cry out. Within a few seconds, she was hustled into the van, the door was slammed shut and the van took off, its light now green. She struggled fiercely, but almost immediately her arms and legs were bound, a wide swath of tape pressed over her lips and a black bag pulled over her head. The van drove only a few blocks until it stopped. She felt herself carried out of it and dumped into the trunk of a car. It sped away.

When she was released from the trunk, her feet were unbound and she was hustled across a concrete floor, through a door and down some steps. She heard another heavy door opening and then slam shut loudly behind her after she was pushed through the doorway. The men around her poked and prodded her body, chuckling with glee and speaking in some foreign tongue. Renate remembered that the young men who had been standing behind her were dark complected and she realized that she had been kidnapped by one of the criminal gangs that had sprung up from the growing Dutch immigrant community. In fact, her captors were from a South Moluccan radical Islamist separatist group. The funds from her sale would go to promote their terrorist activities.

The men took no time in stripping away Renate's clothes, even to her frilly, pink and white socks and clean, white Reeboks. She cried as she felt them cut and pulled away from her body. They were amused by her plump, pale breasts and the fur covered slit between her legs. A rope was looped around her neck and tied off to a pipe in the ceiling. A spreader bar was attached to her ankles. One of the men, apparently the leader, issued a sharp command and the other men ceased their teasing of her. Blinded by the black hood still tied over her head, she heard the basement door open and shut again and found herself alone in the darkness.

Renate did not know how long she stood alone in the damp, chilly basement room. The rope around her neck stretched her so that she had to stand on her tip toes. She was thirsty and afraid. Desperately, she tried to work free her bound wrists behind her, but to no avail. And even if she had managed to free herself, the steel door she had heard slam behind the men was almost certainly going to be an insurmountable obstacle. She prayed and cried while she waited the next development. Her voice was stilled by the tape over her lips or she would have cried out frantically for help. She was intensely conscious of her nakedness. Her mind was going a hundred kilometers an hour. Was she going to be held hostage? Would the men come back and rape her and then kill her? She wanted so much to live. She told God that she would suffer any consequence, endure any condition as long as he saved her from death.

When Renate heard the door to the basement open again, her legs ached terribly. The rope around her neck had grown tighter and tighter as her feet had become tired and she slipped off of her toes again and again. Worse of all, she had to pee.

The voices the girl heard this time were in Dutch.

"Just three hours ago," the voice Renate recognized as the leader was saying as he entered the room. "And no one has touched her."

"Okay, okay," the gruff, accented voice answered. "Her picture and name are all over the news already. Why did you pick such a public place? At least three people saw the snatch."

"Don't worry," the other voice returned. "The van was stolen and no one saw us make the switch to the car. It will be like she vanished into thin air."

The men had completed their approach to the distended girl. She could feel them standing a foot away from her naked body. She was miserable at the thought that she was so ludely displayed for the men. She could feel her ample breasts sway as she shifted her weight, the cool air on her exposed slit between her legs. And what they were saying distressed her. But it was good to know that someone was looking for her. That gave her hope.

A strong, coarse hand grabbed her large, voluptuous left breast. She jumped with a start at the unfamiliar contact. The hand squeezed it gently as if assessing it. Renate whined in protest. The men ignored the hooded girl.

"She has nice tits. That's a good start," the gruff voiced said. He now had both breasts in his hands and he stroked and caressed them until the nipples grew hard. He pinched the stiff, fleshy protuberances, drawing a moan of pain from the girl. She sensed the men walking around her and the hands found her bare rump. They pinched and rubbed it, testing it for firmness. The hands next ran down her thighs, first outside and then in. Renate shook her body in protest, an effort that produced no reaction from the men and only served to draw the noose tighter around her neck. Her hips were assessed and then a finger traced a line up between her rear cheeks and teased the little hole between them. Renate gave out a little hooting protest as she felt the finger play with the delicate ring around the entrance to her bowels. She heard a single word from the gruff voiced man, "Tight."

When the men came back around in front of her, the gruff voiced man requested that the hood be removed. When it had been pulled from her head, Renate stared wide eyed at her assailants, her pleas and protests stilled by the tape over her lips. The gruff voiced man was older, taller and heavier than the brown skinned one. He had short salt and pepper hair, pale skin and wore workman's clothes. The Moluccan was dressed like a college student, jeans and a tee shirt. His skin was smooth and dark and he had long, black hair that touched the tip of his shoulders and a neatly trimmed goatee. His eyes were cruel and hard.

Renate wanted to beg for her release, to let them know that she wouldn't tell anyone what had happened. She would say that she had been lost, that the reports of her kidnapping were a mistake, anything. But the men weren't interested in what their naked, comely prisoner had to say. The gruff voiced man grabbed her face and twisted it right and left. He seemed satisfied. When his hand drifted down her tight belly to the crux between her thighs, Renate knew that she was doomed. All of the rough handling of her flesh had produced an unwanted arousal in her. Never had she thought that he flesh would be the subject of such rude treatment, and her response to it humiliated her. When the man had stroked the inside of her widespread thighs, she had felt her passion rise unwillingly. She knew that now the man would explore her almost virgin sex and that he would find evidence of her shame there. "Why has God put me here?" Renate wondered miserably. "What have I done? Where have I sinned?"

The man's hand found Renate's delicate nether lips amidst the bush of fine, blond hair that covered her loins. She cried out when he pinched them and moaned in frustration and unhappiness when she felt his thick finger part them. "She's wet," the gruff man said.

"All Western women are whores," the dark skinned man said. The gruff voiced man laughed.

"And you think your women are any different?" he said. "Get me one next time and I'll make her writhe and moan for you. In fact, a brown skinned girl might be good. A little diversity. Some men like dark meat."

The Moluccan man replied coldly. "There are some of our women who have lost their way, whose very existence is a defilement. I shall get you one of them. It will be easy. Her brothers will bring her here."

"Her brothers?" the gruff man asked, surprise in his voice. He had his finger deep between the lubricated lips of Renate's cunt and was easing himself deeper and deeper. Renate squirmed and moaned at the invasion, fighting back the growing heat from his ministrations.

"Yes, and that is why the West will be defeated," the young man said. "You are corrupt and vile and permit your women all nature of licentiousness. They deserve to be slaves."

The older man looked up and shrugged his shoulders. "Frankly," he said, "I think life would be very dull if I couldn't watch a pair of pretty legs walking down the street from time to time. And if women are sluts, well that's okay with me."

The man now had two fingers buried deep in Renate's quim. He slid them back and forth while rubbing the edge of his palm over the stiffened button of pleasure above them. Renate felt her breasts grow tight. Her heart was beating heavily in her chest. She didn't want this, hated herself for it, hated the man for what he was doing. She gave out a long sigh as her hips sought to draw her pussy away from the man's reach. The men, hearing her passionate response, looked into her eyes. She could see their lust reflected there in the men's amusement. She jammed her eyes shut to blot it out. She was dreadfully mortified that these strange men's eyes were taking in what no man had ever seen, that her body was giving a response that it had never given. She had read about orgasms and such, but had never had one. Whenever her natural desires had reared their ugly head, she had done as her mother had told her, closed her thighs and prayed to God. Even so, now, when she felt the surge of pleasure in her loins, she knew that she was about to have one.

"Mmmmmmmmmmm! Mmmmmmmmmmm!" she exclaimed through her taped lips as the pleasure coursed through her. "No! No!" her mind screamed. Her thighs twitched, her hips pressed her cunt forwards into the man's hand. "Mmmmmmmmm! Mmmmmmmmmmmmm!" she called out. She was crying and coming at the same time. And then her bladder released. The man pulled his hand back sharply as the yellow fluids poured out of her. The girl moaned in misery. She hadn't wanted to pee. She had known she was close to bursting, but the men gave her no chance to ask for relief. She felt the warmth of her discharge flow down her thighs and heard it splatter on the cement floor under her feet.

The gruff man reared his hand back and slapped the girl viciously across the face. "You pig!" he yelled at her. He slapped her again and again. Renate had never been hit like this before. The pain and shock of the blows stunned her. Her misery was increased tenfold at the man's insulting invective. The thin, brown skinned man held back the other man's hand before he could land a fourth blow.

"When you own her, you can beat her," he said.

The angry, older man glared at Renate. His blows to her face had caused the rope around her neck to tighten and she was beginning to choke. He watched as her face grew red and her eyes began to bulge.

"And if she chokes to death," the man said, "there's no deal."

The younger man stepped forwards and loosened the rope around Renate's neck. She took a deep, relieved breath through her nose. Tears flowed down her face. Her mind was trying to register what she had just heard. This man was going to buy her. He would own her and then beat her.

He would abuse her, rape her. She realized that God had fulfilled her prayer. She wasn't going to die. At least not yet. The thought entered her mind that she might live to regret the answer to her supplications.

But that was many months ago. Renate was gone. She was Klara now. She had quickly acclimated herself to routine, callous sexual abuse. The gruff man had beaten and raped her, but afterwards he sold her to someone else. She lost track of how long she was bound, gagged and hooded before she ended up in this god forsaken country. They had given her a new name and beat her when she failed to respond to it. They had forced their cocks down her throat until she learned to accept them without choking and gagging. They had used all of her entrances brutally and at their whims, insisting that she exhibit an authentic and enthusiastic, lustful response.

Klara had been surprised how quickly she learned her lessons. She had become addicted to the pleasure her body could give her and learned to fuck with unfeigned enthusiasm. She had known back in high school that she had sinned when she had allowed that boy to penetrate her, to make her impure, and now she was being punished. And part of her punishment was to experience the shame and debasement that her sexual pleasure brought her.

It had been harder to get used to the fact that her body was constantly on display for all to see. It didn't matter that all of the other slave girls were naked too. Her stomach still soured with shame when one of the masters stared at her nakedness lustfully, eyeing her available breasts, the hairless, naked lips of her sex. And the constant nakedness, along with the bright colored brand of a fire breathing dragon that she bore on her belly and the marks above her chest that denoted her new name, marked her as a class of being wholly separate and apart from other women. She saw all the other pretty, young girls, their bare bellies marked with ferocious lions, bears, snakes and other beasts, their bare, pinkish skin, the voluptuousness of their flesh and thought, "I am one of them." When she watched while one of the other naked women accepted a master's thick cock between her lips or opened her thighs to receive the man's hot meat, she thought, "I am one of them." When she knelt silently in a room unoccupied but for the patient, servile slave girls awaiting a command from a master, their naked breasts raised in presentation, their thighs spread wide invitingly, she thought, "I am one of them."

There were women on the estate who were not slaves. There were the heavy, merry, peasant women who served in the kitchen or who cleaned the mansion. They looked upon the slave girls with disdain and mockery. They expressed themselves with ribaldry when the slave girls lined up to pick up the trays of food to be delivered about the estate or taken to the Lord's dining room or the staff refectory. Sometimes, when work in the kitchen was slow, they would capture some hapless slave girl and make her serve their needs. Klara had more than once been forced to kneel between their fat thighs and lick their mushy cunts. Most of the female peasant staff were older, but there were a few that were young enough to have maintained their girlish shapes and fine skin. These were the ones who treated the slave girls most cruelly, slapping and whipping them, reporting them to the masters for infractions. But it was their cold, disdainful looks that hurt most, as if these attractive young women would not have succumbed as they had when subjected to the cruelties of their slave training.

But there also was something liberating about her constant nakedness. She had no pretenses to shed. She was what she was. And there was pride in her comeliness despite her shame. Each day, the slave girls were required to put in at least an hour of physical training in a special basement room in the mansion devoted to that purpose. There was a slave mistress, a slave herself, but somewhat older than the other girls, who kept the records and whipped the girls who failed, for whatever reason, to comply. A girl might have been locked in a cage for three days by one of the masters, but she would still receive her punishment. Klara worked out diligently, wanting to keep her body trim and appetizing for her master. She worked at decorating her face to highlight her pretty, blue eyes, redden her plump, enticing lips.

Although the slave girls were an abject class of human, devoid of rights, there was something worse. Klara, of course, knew of the ponygirls. One could not avoid them. She watched with horrid fascination as the hooded, ponytailed, naked, former women toiled on the long, wide dirt track, pulling their carts. They frightened her. They were faceless beings, shaped like human women, large and strong, fitted with high, black leather boots. They peed and shat right out in the open like animals. They often bore the remnants of a whipping on their body. She could see the track and the door to the pony barn from her master's bedroom window on the second floor of the carriage house and she watched with fascination as the sweaty, silent creatures were led about their duties by their callous trainers. Klara might be a slave girl, but she could laugh and cry. She could smile at a master, use her hands to feed herself and touch her own body. She could speak, if only when spoken to. And, when the masters weren't around or weren't looking, she could kiss and caress her fellow slaves, enjoying their bodies and obtaining comfort and warmth in their arms. No, she didn't ever want to be made into a ponygirl. She would rather die.

Klara belonged to Jake, but, as a slave girl, she could never disobey another master's order. Jake reserved her for his own use, although when she had arrived he had loaned her to the lord of the estate for several days. The man, who she came to know as Burnham, had savagely misused her and kept her confined to a tiny cage when not in actual use. Since then, most of the men, especially Jake's men, had respected his ownership rights. His name was stamped on the golden discs that dangled from the bottom of her nether lips. But from time to time, as she scurried around the estate on various tasks, one of the men would order her to her knees and demand obeisance. She would caress them skillfully and hurriedly, lest her master witness her degradation. She feared that if she saw her opening her lips or thighs to another master without his permission he would be angry with her, reject her as despoiled. On the other hand, if she refused, she would be beaten severely for disobeying a master's order and she worried that he would abandon her if he felt that she was unruly. She had never said anything to her master about it. But she always made sure that afterwards she cleaned herself thoroughly before presenting herself to his service.

As Klara toted the heavy tray across the lawn to the main building, one of the masters came towards her from the other direction. Klara saw him staring at her as he approached from a distance. As he came closer and closer, she sensed his desire for her. She bent her head and drew in her shoulders in an attempt to discourage the man's lustful intentions. As he neared her, he called out to her, "Stop, slave."

Klara had known almost no English when she had been captured. She had learned some simple English commands during her training, enough for her to understand what sexual service was being demanded or how to position her body for her master's pleasure. She had learned much more since being with Jake, but still missed many words. These she knew. She stopped immediately, immobilized by the man's voice. He was wearing the black tee shirt of the security men. The shirt had an outline in red of the fiendish hound that served as the estate's symbol over the left part of the chest. The man's face was lean and cruel looking. He was thin, but strong. He carried an automatic rifle over his shoulder and a riding crop hooked into his belt. Fearfully, Klara awaited his next command.

"Put down the tray," he ordered in a churlish voice. Klara complied immediately. The man had one of the standard slave gags in his hand. "Open your mouth," he ordered. When Klara complied, he thrust the thick wedge of leather between her trembling lips and fastened the buckle behind her head. Klara's large breasts pressed against the man's chest as he reached around her. Why he wanted her gagged, she did not know. But she could tell that something bad was about to happen. She looked at the riding crop on his belt and thought unhappily that she was going to be beaten. She could think of nothing that she had done wrong. But the man didn't need a reason.

The man ordered the slave girl to follow him. She did so dutifully, but wondered why he kept looking furtively around him. He would know that Jake was away. He was with security. Maybe he was afraid someone would betray his abuse of her to her master and feared confrontation? It was still dinner time around the estate and there didn't seem to be anyone else about. The man led her around the corner of the main building. There was a car parked there with two men sitting in it. As they neared the car, the trunk popped open. The security guard turned to Klara and ordered her to present her back to him. He deftly locked her leather bracelets behind her back. He then pulled her towards the open trunk, and pushed her in. Klara, panicking, tried to call out as she felt herself forced into the trunk, but the gag stifled her cry. The man's hands connected the rings on her ankle bracelets together and pulled a black bag over her head which he tightened at the neck with a drawstring. He took a clasp and fastened the rings on the ankle bracelets to those on Klara's wrists, hogtieing her. The trunk slammed shut and the car's engine revved. It quickly pulled away.

* * * * * * * * * * * * * *

Drabik was in a happy mood. He had just left the little inn where he and Anna had their *tête-à-tête's*. It had been a particularly pleasurable encounter. He loved the gang lord's daughter's smooth, pale skin set off by her long, jet back hair. She had plush, but firm breasts that aroused him when he sucked at her teats. Her legs were long and strong and she gripped him tightly with them around his back when he entered her. She had an eager, skilled mouth that made him moan with pleasure. She was a wanton, lustful creature.

But that was not what made the afternoon long session so exciting. It was the fact that she had spent the entire afternoon dressed as a ponygirl.

He had first started acclimating the slut to the pleasures of bondage months ago. She had started out protesting vigorously as he had bound her and forced her to submit to his wanton use of her body. It was then that he had first taught the young lady to swallow his cum, a thing she did religiously now and with pleasure.

He now used her ass as often as he used her cunt. And he made her stand for long times submissively, trembling, her eyes begging for use. For he often gagged her, either with a ring gag so that he could explore her mouth and throat at will, or with one of the thick leather plugs that the slave girls wore with a wide leather shield over her lips and chin. He had even whipped her, although he had gone lightly, not wanting to scare her off. Just enough to get her blood to boil. But today had been a first. Today, for the first time, she had agreed, reluctantly, to wear a ponygirl hood.

She was already there, kneeling on the bed, her clothes stripped from her body when he entered the small, cozy room at the preappointed time. The bed was a large four poster with a soft, plush mattress.

"Hello, lover," she said to him as he walked in the door. She had a bottle of vodka next to the bed on a nightstand and she had already apparently imbibed. Her eyes were just a little glassy and her smile just a little loose. Her naked breasts swayed as she leaned over to pour Drabik a shot. She handed it to him and said playfully, "Your ponygirl awaits."

Drabik said nothing. He took the shot glass and threw the fiery substance down his throat. He put the glass down and set the overnight bag he was holding down on the floor. He leaned over and zipped it open producing two thick leather bracelets. "Turn around," was all he said.

Anya grinned lustfully and turned her back to him. Without instruction, she placed her arms behind her and accepted without struggle the application of the confinements on her wrists. When they were on, Drabik locked them together behind her back. "Bend over," he ordered, and Anya bent at the waist, crushing her breasts against her graceful thighs. "Spread your legs," he said as he placed his hands on her tight rear cheeks. Anya pushed her knees wide and her black hair covered slit made itself available to Drabik's hand.

When Drabik covered Anya's mons with his hand, she sighed with pleasurable anticipation. "Oh, yes, Anton," she said. "Yessssss," she uttered softly as he spread her nether lips with his fingers and delved into her already moist slit.

"Ohhhhhh, Anton, what you do to me," she moaned as Drabik massaged the little button at the apex of her pussy. "I'm your fuck slave, Anton. Fill me with your cock, I'm ready for you."

"But you're not dressed, Anya," Drabik responded, more than a hint of contempt in his voice. He reached down into his bag and withdrew a ponygirl collar from it. "Here's your collar, ponygirl," he said as he brushed her long black hair off of her pale, white back and presented it to her neck. The ponygirl collars were made of leather covered hard plastic and covered the whole neck. The front was higher than the back and kept the pony's head pointed slightly upwards, ideal for a creature bent forwards, pulling her load. This gave the ponies a clear view of the track ahead.

Anya had to raise her head so that the pony collar could be affixed. A shudder went through her body as it clicked shut. A long, thick strap hung from the back of the collar and Drabik hooked her bound wrists to it. "Turn around," Drabik ordered. "I have something new for you."

Anya obediently turned on the bed. Her head was poised upwards and she looked lustfully up at the tall, dark, ponygirl trainer. Drabik raised his hand and showed her his surprise. It was a blue, neoprene, ponygirl hood. He had never hooded her. But each time they met in this second floor bedroom of the small inn, he tried to push the arrogant, haughty, spoiled woman a little further.

When Anya saw the hood her eyes went wide. She loved the little games she played with her lover. Once, when she had watched Drabik fuck the ponygirl Lightning, after a round of abuse that she had egged on, she had challenged Drabik to 'fuck her like a ponygirl'. When Drabik had taken her up on it several months ago, tying her up and ruthlessly fucking her throat, she had experienced a sexual thrill beyond her wildest dreams. Since then, she fantasized constantly about being dominated by her father's hit man. She had allowed him to put on a collar, to make her wear the tall, heavy ponygirl boots, gag her. But she had never worn a ponygirl hood. She wasn't sure she wanted to. How close could she go to the reality of being a ponygirl, a status much to be feared in real life, without losing her mind? "N,no, Anton," she pleaded hesitatingly. "I don't want to wear a hood, please?" Her protest was almost an entreaty.

"Come on, Anya," Drabik said, presenting the soft, blue fabric to her, rubbing it on her face. "Just once. For me."

He sat on the bed next to the trembling woman. She knew that Drabik was a man to be feared. How much should she put him in her control? What if he refused to take it off? He could march her out the door and down the stairs. Once he had placed a tattoo on her belly and shaved her nether lips, no one would be able to tell who she was. She would look like all the other ponygirls. He could take her to the barn and let all the other men fuck her. And then what? Sell her? Stick her in front of a cart and make her pull him around? She thought not.

"No, Anton,' she said more forcefully. "No hood. Don't do it, please." Her forcefulness had turned plaintive. Drabik began to softly caress her swelling breasts.

"Come on, Anya," he whispered into her ear as he stimulated her. "Just this once. If you don't like it, I'll take it off. I promise."

The svelte woman's pussy was lush with her arousal. Drabik's hand slipped between her thighs and he slid his fingers inside her. "You'll love it, Anya. I'm sure of it. Just this once."

Suddenly, the thought of being hooded and anonymous sent a thrill through the impassioned woman. "What would it be like?" she thought. Her breath had become heavy, her hands twisted in their confinements behind her. "Okay, Anton," she whispered. "Just once. But you'll take it off when I say so?" she asked.

"Of course, Anya," Drabik replied. "What do you think I am?"

Usually, the neoprene hood of a ponygirl was applied over a head that had been closely shaved except for the skein of hair that would constitute the ponytail. Drabik had no plans to shave Anya's beautiful long, straight, black hair from her. After all, how could she hide that once she went back to her role as lusty daughter of the lord of the estate. But the hood was flexible and would stretch sufficiently to cover her hair. He grabbed the panting woman's hair behind her head and passed it through the small hole at the back of the ponygirl hood located near the top. Drabik had hooded many a ponygirl and he had no trouble managing this. When the hair was pulled through, he expanded the stretchable hood and began to pull it down over Anya's head. She gasped as it came down over her face. Drabik adjusted it so that it lay flat against her facial contours and then attached its tiny eyelets to hooks on the top of the collar. He leaned back to take a look at his creation, the now anonymous face.

"You make a pretty ponygirl, Anya," he said, smiling. "It's a natural."

Anya took a moment to adjust her vision. The hood had dime sized openings for her eyes and she had to turn her head to see her lover. "Oh, Anton," she said nervously. "I don't know, I can't see."

Drabik took his hand and softly covered the blue hooded female's mouth. "Shhhhhh!" he whispered. "Ponygirls don't talk."

He had laid on the bed next to him a slave gag and he deftly seized it with his other hand. Before the nervous woman knew what was happening, he pushed the thick leather plug between her lips and thrust it home. The hood left a wide opening for the ponygirl's mouth so that she could be properly gagged or her mouth used for its only real purpose. Anya's eyes widened in fright. But Drabik couldn't see them. They were hidden behind the soft, neoprene material. She recorded her shock by a wave of her head. "Ooooomfpf" she called out as she tried to fight off the thick plug. But Drabik quickly locked the gag behind her head, covering her lips and chin with the leather shield attached.

Anya began to moan and whine in protest. He had tricked her. He promised to remove it if she asked him to, but now there was no way that she could. She tried to scream her objections, but the sound came out muffled and distorted. Drabik grabbed the woman's stiff nipples and twisted them harshly. Anya moaned in pain. "You make a pretty little ponygirl, Anya, but you have to obey me or you'll be whipped," he threatened in a stern, harsh voice. "Do you want to be whipped, Anya? I can do that too. I brought the whip." Drabik reached down to his bag and withdrew a long, leather covered rattan cane. "I'll mark you where no one will be able to se it, Anya. No one, that is, except for the pretty little slave girls that you like to fuck. What will they think if they see their mistress all covered with welts, eh Anya? They'll think that you're a slut, and they will be right," he told her. "You are a whorish slut, aren't you?"

The pain from the twisting of her nipples caused Anya's body to stiffen. But when Drabik released them, she realized that her pussy was growing hotter and hotter. She wanted Drabik to fuck her, hood or no hood. She looked at him pleadingly. But the facial expressions of ponygirls can't be seen.

"Let me put your boots on, ponygirl," Drabik said. He pulled Anya's legs out from under her until they dangled off of the side of the bed. Taking the heavy, black boots from his bag, he laced them up on Anya's feet. When he was done, he pulled her up by the ring in the front of her collar. There was a full length mirror on the back of the closet in the room and Drabik guided the lustful young woman towards it.

"See how you look, Anya? Doesn't it make you hot?"

Anya had to peer carefully through the little holes in the hood, but when she focused, she could see herself clearly in the mirror. "Oh, god," she thought, "just like a ponygirl." She could see her hardened breasts, the flushness of her chest, the slickness of her plump nether lips. The only thing that spoiled the picture was the thick thatch of curly black hair that covered her loins. She would never agree to have that shaved, she thought. And then a fearful thought went through her head. "He wouldn't do it against my will, would he?"

Drabik looked leeringly into the mirror at his creation. He reached around and placed his hands on Anya's hard beasts and caressed them. "Like what you see, Anya?" He slid his hand down and probed her hot, dilated womb. Anya was overcome with passion. She melted when she felt the hand stroke her fevered slit. "Fuck me!' Oh, god, fuck me!" she tried to say through the thick leather probe that filled her mouth. Drabik pulled her away from the mirror and pushed her to the floor.

"Ponygirls don't get fucked on beds, Anya," he said to her. "Now spread your legs and get ready for my cock!"

Anya lay on her back, her legs splayed widely, awaiting her lover's pleasure. Her arms were crushed behind her, but she paid it no mind. She watched feverishly while Drabik slowly removed his clothes. When he was naked, his thick manhood jutting out proudly, he sank to his knees between her outstretched thighs. He leaned over and rubbed his rigid pole the length of her steaming slit. Her body twitched and she moaned with expectation. When he slid his piece home within her, her lust exploded.

"Mmmmmmmpf! Mmmmmmmmpf", she cried out as wave after wave of pleasure shot through her. Her legs jerked and spasmed as her pussy throbbed and convulsed. Drabik was taking long, deliberate strokes within her, letting his own lust slowly build. When the bound and hooded imitation ponygirl's mind wrenching pulses of pleasure slowed, he ratcheted up his pace, building her up to another climax.

Anya dug her booted heels hard into the floor and thrust her hips back at her tormentor. She squeezed her pussy's muscles tightly endeavoring to capture the hard wand that was priming her lust. Her mind wanted him to stop, the waves of excruciating sensation overwhelming her power to think, but her body wanted more, more, more.

When the fearsome ponygirl trainer had driven her past her third wrenching explosion of lust, he was ready to achieve his own satisfaction. He placed his strong arms beneath her thighs and pushed her knees up to her chest. His cock was heavy with the irrational woman's discharge and he slid it free of her sheath, grabbing it with his hand and pointing it at a smaller, tighter target. Its bulbous head forced the tight ring of flesh open easily. He pushed himself within her as the small circle of muscle gripped him firmly. He plunged into her bowels, feeling the hot moistness envelope him. Anya shuddered and groaned as she felt herself invaded. Drabik cried out as his cock began to throb and pulse, shooting his hot cum deep within her. He thrust harder and harder as he emptied his aching balls. He stared down at the blue hooded creature under him, pleased at his mastery of the slut. He had learned about Anya's little escapade with his favorite ponygirl, Lightning. He had vowed to make the jealous Russian girl pay.

When Drabik had fully satisfied himself, he rose to his feet. Anya lay limp on the floor. He went to the bed and poured himself another shot of vodka. And then another. The warmth of the fiery liquor spread through him. He went to the bathroom and cleaned his equipment of Anya's wastes and returned to the bedroom. Anya had not moved. Her body was covered with a sheen of sweat and her chest still rose and fell quickly. He picked up the whip and gave the bound girl a fierce blow across her breasts. Anya screamed with the unexpected pain and curled her body defensively.

"On your knees, ponygirl," Drabik ordered sternly, "unless you want another stroke of the cane."

Anya rapidly rose to her knees in fearful panic. She was at his absolute mercy now. Her heart leapt with joy at the sensation. Due to the limitations of vision of the hood, she could not see all of her lover's body, but she could see his hand idly caressing his now limp cock, and she wanted it.

"Come closer, whore," Drabik spat. Anya crept closer to him until her body was between his outstretched legs. He reached behind her shrouded, blue clad head and undid her gag. When the thick plug of leather was pulled from her mouth, she spoke lowly, her lips brushing the tip of Drabik's fat cock. "Oh, Anton," she moaned, "that was unreal. I can't believe it."

Drabik grabbed her cheeks forcefully with his heavy hand. "No talking, ponygirl, or I'll have to whip you again. Now open your mouth and suck my cock. And you better be good."

Anya nodded her head. She spread her lips and enveloped the long, limp meat. She breathed in the sweat of his loins and almost fainted. She would be good, she thought, better than that slut of a pony he likes to fuck. "It'll be me he dreams of, me he'll want! And I want him again and again!" As she felt the manhood begin to harden in her mouth, she sighed with growing lust.

* * * * * * * *** * * * *

It was the vision of the anonymous blue head stroking his cock that Drabik had on his mind when he descended the stairs to the basement of the Grobgy mansion. He had spilled himself down the faux ponygirl's throat, holding her head pinned to his belly by her long, black ponytail. A wave of pleasure went through him as he thought of it. When he reached the steel door at the bottom of the stairs, he shook free of the happy memory and redirected himself to the business ahead. He passed through the door using his master key and walked down to another heavy, steel door half way down the corridor. He unlocked the door and entered.

Tonight he hoped to find out what was behind the schemes of Michael Burnham and his enforcer Jake Barnes. Drabik had met Jake at a party the night after Lightning had won the championship and he had easily spotted him as a man of hardness and superiority. He was posing as Burnham's bodyguard, but Drabik knew that that was just a front right away. Men like he and Jake had an eye for men of their own kind. Drabik had had a connection of his investigate the small, but imposing man. The word had come back that Jake Barnes was a fixer, a very capable and feared one who had done dirt on almost every continent. Tonight he hoped to find out what dirt he was up to in Kalikastan.

The blond haired slave girl was strung with her wrists in the air, her bracelets connected by a chain to a hook in the ceiling. Two equally naked, sweaty, crude looking men were lolling about the small room. It was nothing fancy. It was windowless and had bare, blue-gray, cinderblock walls and a rough concrete floor. A single, bright light bulb covered by a wire screen illuminated the room and it cast huge, dark shadows of the men and their helpless victim on the walls. There were two, long benches and a table that held a variety of evil looking instruments. This was not a training room. It was for punishments.

The girl dangling on her toes and moaning her fear and pain was Jake Barnes' favorite slut, Klara. Drabik had his spies almost everywhere and he had had a full report of the American's doings since the night of the party. Men were likely to be careless when they spoke around creatures that were considered as little more than pets. He knew that slave girls heard almost everything that was said around them. It was a necessary defensive measure since they needed to know when something evil and painful was being planned for them. And a missed order might lead to very painful discipline. He was sure that this slave girl, who he had ordered kidnapped and brought here to the Grobgy mansion, could tell him a lot about what was really up.

So far, no one had asked the pitiful, big breasted slave girl anything. She bore the red stripes that were evidence of a vociferous whipping. There was a blindfold over her eyes and Drabik could see that it was wet with her tears. The men who had been tormenting her had taken a break, but she was still uttering a low, continuous moan through her ring gagged mouth. A ring gag allowed an abused slave girl to vent her full vocal dismay at her excruciating torture. She could hear her own loud, piteous moans and wails echo through the room. But she could not form any words to beg for mercy or ask for forgiveness for her transgression.

The men had been instructed not to conduct any interrogation of the slave girl until she had been properly 'warmed up'. She had arrived in the night in the trunk of the Mercedes that Drabik had dispatched. A simple bribe had convinced one of Burnham's security men to facilitate her abduction. She had spent the evening locked in a cage, bound, hooded and gagged. She had not been fed and had been prevented from sleeping by shocks delivered on a regular basis by an electrified dildo that had been shoved rudely up her pussy and kept in place by a belt that went around her waist.

One of the hazards of a prolonged torture session was that the passions of the men would overload and the carefully measured delivery of violence would be compromised by fevered lust. Death or serious injury to the subject could result. So there was always another slave girl kept in the room whose job was to modulate the fever that was always brought on by the abuse of the female subject. A shapely, naked, young slave girl with long, brown hair was kneeling on the floor servicing the cock of one of the torturers. She cast a terrified, sidelong glance at Drabik when he entered, but did not pause in her expert oral service to the man. There was always the chance that she could find herself strung up in place of the victim if she faltered in her duties, or even just for fun when the torment of the other slave girl was through. Drabik noted that the slave girl was new and made a mental note to himself to try her out very soon.

The men who had been tormenting the pretty blond girl for hours were experts at their tasks. This was the end of the girl's second two hour session, a prolonged break having been taken for lunch. Drabik was sure that the girl was primed. He stepped up to her and removed her blindfold. Her body shuddered when he approached her and her sapphire eyes widened with fear as she saw the scarred face of the deadly criminal.

Klara stared in terror at the cruel looking man in front of her. She had been tortured and whipped during her slave training and had suffered the lash a number of times since then. But that was nothing like what she had undergone today. Nothing in the surreal, random world in which she had lived since her capture many months ago had prepared her for this. Her ears still rang with the echoes of her frantic screams as the lash had riven her flesh. She had no idea why this ordeal had been visited on her other than as a punishment for her sins. Perhaps God had seen that she had lost her repentance at her youthful transgression at giving away her maidenhead. She had become too enamored of her master, too willing to give in to bodily pleasures. Of course she would be punished. She deserved it. But she couldn't help but beg and plead that the travail of her chastisement be lifted. She screamed and wailed as she was beaten, slapped, punched and kicked. Her body was a checkerboard of bruises. And when she looked into the fearsome eyes of this devilish man who stood before her, she knew that he ordeal was not over. Her sweaty, pain wracked body shuddered.

Drabik enjoyed the girl's dismay. Her fear made her large breasts tremble and sway as her body shook. She was making little 'ga-ga' sounds through the ring gag. A river of tears flowed from each pretty eye. He took hold of her long, thick, stiff nipples and teased them. The girl jumped as her breasts registered the pain which resulted from the contact, pain brought on by the bruising left by the earlier torture of the points of her breasts. Drabik smiled as he noted her sensitivity. He spoke to her.

"Slave, I am going to ask you some questions. You are going to answer them. If you give any answers that I don't like, I will bring you immediate, excruciating pain. Do you understand?"

Drabik had been informed that the girl's English was weak, but that she was conversant in Dutch and German. Drabik spoke German fluently, as well as several other languages. There would be no communication problem.

Klara nodded her head vociferously. She didn't know what knowledge she might possibly have that this man would want to know, but she was willing to give all of it up. She would do anything to avoid more pain.

"You are the property of a man called Jake, is that true?" Drabik asked her.

Klara looked at the man intently. Was this about Jake, her master? Yes, she was his property. Was that all they wanted to know? She nodded her head in affirmation.

"Good," Drabik replied. "Now you are going to tell me everything that you know about this Jake, everything. Everything he has ever said, everything that you ever heard said to him. Do you understand?"

Now Klara realized what was up. This was a test from God. Everything had been taken away from her, her will, her dignity, her personhood. The only thing that she had left was her loyalty and love for her master, as strange as that may be. He used her as a whore, satisfied his lusts on her. But he had saved her from that other house where she had been introduced as a slave. He protected her and, in his way, she believed, he loved her. To betray his kindness would be an evil thing. She would not sin again. She would never tell this man anything about her master. She would rather die.

Before Klara could communicate an answer, there came another question. "Have you ever heard him talk about a ponygirl called *Molnya*?" Drabik asked her menacingly. It was a voice that had been the last sound heard by many men and a number of women too. Drabik was democratic when it came to dealing death.

The woefully frightened slave girl shook her head 'no'. She closed her eyes and began to cry again. She realized that she had just condemned herself to more intolerable misery.

Drabik could tell right away that the girl was lying. Well, maybe she needed more persuasion. He stepped back to the table behind him and removed two small belts. He approached the dismal slave girl. "I don't take to whores that lie to me, slave girl. I'm going to beat your breasts in a moment. First, I'm going to tie them up nicely so that they make better targets. When they pump up with your trapped blood they will begin to swell and ache. And then I'm going to lash them with the riding crop. After that, I'll give you another chance to answer the question."

The dark slaver fixed the belts around Klara's ample tits. She winced with pain when he tightened them harshly around the base. They immediately began to swell and ache. Her eyes looked pleadingly at her tormentor. How could she make him understand, she thought frantically. She couldn't answer him. She just couldn't!

Drabik lit himself a cigarette and sat on the bench. The brown haired slave girl had completed her task with the guard's cock and was kneeling near him on the floor submissively awaiting her next command. Drabik seized her thin, long hair behind her head and pulled her to him. He read her name stenciled in 2" high blue letters on her chest. 'Fiona'. Not her free name, of course, but a slave name, one she would answer to from now on. She had broad, plump lips and thin, dark, brown eyebrows. Her pert, firm breasts were blessed with wide areolas and stiff, long, thin nipples. Her skin was dark, almost Mediterranean. Drabik took a long, laconic drag on his cigarette and considered her. He wondered idly how many slave girls he had fucked since coming to Kalikastan. Hundreds? How many of them did he really remember? It had been an easy shift from the war ravaged mountains of Afghanistan to the wide, rolling plains of this East European country. He and his men had been given carte blanche when seizing a hostile village there. The girls and young women there were fierce and beautiful. It was where he first learned to take pleasure from administering pain to a female. It was the only way to get them to fuck. And even then, you had better not put your dick in their mouths without a ring gag. A couple of his men had learned that lesson the hard way.

Drabik was marking his time until Klara's breasts started to balloon up. They would turn purple and swell painfully. She would flinch at a mere touch before he administered the whip.

One of the guards had gone behind the frantic blond haired girl and had spread her rear cheeks. The slave girl's eyes filled with unhappiness as the man eased his thick, hard cock into her narrow rear hole. Drabik didn't interfere. He enjoyed the sound of her squeals as the man forced the passage. It would give the girl something to do while she awaited the continuation of her torment. He released the brown haired girl's hair and pushed her over his knee. She spread her legs obediently, giving him access to her plump, hairless sex. He thrust his thick fingers into her already sopping channel. It smelled of use. While he watched Klara endure her anal assault, he idly played with the brown haired slave's pussy, making her squirm and pant as he raised her lust.

It only took a few minutes for Klara's breasts to begin to turn a dark purple. They looked like two plump, ripe, fruit on her chest. The man behind her finished with a loud groan and a final, powerful thrust into her bowels. Timing was everything.

The deadly slave master rose from the bench and let the brown haired girl slip to the floor. He went to the table and selected a three foot long reed encased in leather.

Klara had obviously received no enjoyment from the assault on her nether region. She looked a miserable sight. Her long, wavy, blond hair was all tangled and stringy with dirt and sweat from her captivity and her ordeal. There were dark, almost purple rings under her bright blue eyes which were red rimmed and bloodshot. Her breasts were set to explode from their confinement, offset from her chest like huge plums. Her torso and legs were striped with long, red wounds.

Drabik flicked his finger at her right breast and the girl jumped with pain. Her forlorn eyes pleaded with Drabik for mercy and she made a little "ooooooooouing" sound from her rounded and distended lips. Drabik smiled at her, stepped to the side and reared his hand back, the whip fully extended. The other men stood to the sides of Drabik, set to enjoy the spectacle of the girl's torture.

When the whip landed across Klara's breasts, it gave out a loud 'whack!' The firmness of the ballooned up breasts caused the whip to bounce back after it struck. Klara's legs gave out under her as her body recorded the fierce pain. "Oooooooooooooo!" she called out piteously as she slumped in the chains, her hands held tightly above her. Drabik slowly brought his whip hand back again and then, swiftly, delivered another agonizing blow. "Oooooooooooouuuu!" Klara screamed. She had never experienced pain like this before. Her conscious mind shut down and her reactive mind took over. When she saw the whip going back a third time, she began to blubber and sob, her distressed mind unable to form any words. "Whack!" the third blow landed between the other two. "Oooooooooouu! Oooooooooouuuu!" the poor girl screamed.

The naked guards on either side of Drabik gazed with intent lust as they watched the female form abused. They were both stroking their hardened manhoods, their muscular bodies gleaming with sweat. The naked brown haired girl trembled with fear as she beheld the cruelty of the men who held her in thrall. She pitied the poor girl who was the object of the ferocity, and thanked providence that it was not her. She made a note to herself to obey these men in everything they asked with alacrity and joy, regardless of what it was.

The small room echoed with Klara's sobs. Drabik paused in his abuse of her to let her torment sink in. He ordered one of the men to tighten the chain that held her wrists and hands aloft. When the pitiable girl had slumped, her knees unable to lock as a result of the effects of her torment, her feet had started to drag on the floor. The man pulled on the end of the chain until she was elevated above the floor, her big toes just barely touching the cold, hard cement beneath her.

"*Zwei mehr*, Klara," Drabik informed her in German. Two more. The girl looked up at the use of her name. Somehow, the use of her name made the cruel intentions of the hard looking man more personal. Falling back into English, she tried to form the words 'No, please don't', but the sound that emerged from her mouth was a mumbled, distorted "Oooooooeeeeeeeaseoooooooon't!" She swung her feet futilely, trying to gain purchase on the floor. "Ooooooooooo! Eeeeeeeeease!" she called out.

Drabik was happy. He had her talking. That was the first step. He swung his arm back and released the whip on the top of the near to bursting purple orbs. Klara's body jerked and twisted as the pain ran tore through her like a bullet. "Oooooooouuuuu! Ooooooooooo! Eeeeeeeeeease!" the men heard. Drabik had saved the most savage blow for last. It would be the one she would remember best. "Whack!" The leather encased reed met the poor girl's swollen flesh with brute force. Klara's eyes rolled back in her head. Her body could not summon up the will to respond other than to emit a low, piteous moan through her distended lips.

The heinously cruel killer allowed the girl to recover from her excruciating ordeal. One of the men slapped him on the back and expressed his admiration for the man's expert administration of torment. As if recalling her existence, the men looked around at the pretty, brown haired girl who was still kneeling on the floor, her hands tucked behind her, her back straight, her pretty breasts presented to her masters. She was crying and her body was shaking. The men laughed. One of the guards, his thick, hard cock still in his hand, motioned her to her feet. He ordered her to bend over and place her hands on the bench. The girl complied instantly and spread her legs without need for instruction. The guard took his place behind her and pressed his cock between the folds of her hairless pussy and thrust himself in. The other guard went around to the other side of the bench and forced his steely rod between the girl's ready lips. The room filled with the grunts and groans of the three.

Drabik's meat was as hard as a rock, but he would bide his time for satisfaction. This was business and he needed to get the information from the girl before the effects of her torture wore off and her resolve reformed. Not that he didn't have a variety of additional means at his disposal to inflict excruciating pain, but he really didn't want to waste the time.

In the end, once she had returned to a fully conscious state, and after Drabik had removed the thick, round, ring gag from her mouth, the girl told Drabik everything that she could remember about her master and his friends. She described Martinez and Curley, Leon and Tucker. She begged Drabik's pardon as she swore that she had little English and could not understand everything that they said. Crying and sobbing at her betrayal of her master, her failure before God to keep her oath, she told the dark man who had tortured her beyond her endurance that she had heard the name '*Molnya*' many times and that the men had also spoken of someone named Maddy. She told how she had been gifted to Jake on one of his trips to buy ponygirls for the lord of the estate. She had heard the name Burnham. She described the lord of the estate and told about the chocolate ponygirl she had seen. It was all she really knew.

When Drabik had exhausted his questioning of the unhappy girl, he put the whip back down on the table. He released the straps around the girl's purple breasts and she screamed in pain as her blood began to circulate once again. He took a length of chain and, bending down, affixed it to the girl's right ankle, connecting it to the ring on the leather bracelet there. Klara hung limply at the end of her chain. Her heart was heavy with guilt at her loss of what she saw as her last chance at salvation. She knew that she would never see her master again. She couldn't face him now, anyhow. She felt that she deserved to die and, looking at the evil man before her prayed that he would just finish her off, slit her throat, beat her until she was dead. But when she felt her right leg being lifted into the air, her resolve dissipated again.

Drabik had passed the free end of the chain through a ring in the ceiling and had drawn the girl's right leg upwards. He legs now hung splayed wide open in a vertical split, revealing her naked, plump nether lips between them. Klara's eyes peered at him piteously. Her lips were free and she could plead and beg for mercy at will, but she did not. Her lips trembled with fear at what new abuse was to be visited on her. The fact that she had told the man everything that she knew was irrelevant, she knew that. This was a man who loved to inflict pain. Well, she thought miserably, she deserved it. Maybe he would kill her. That would be fine.

Klara's free leg swung free an inch above the floor and Drabik took a small chain and anchored it to a ring in the concrete. He wanted her nice and still for this next part. He took a heavy set of metal cutters from the table behind him and approached the distended girl. Klara whined when she saw the fierce implement. He was going to cut her, slice her open a piece at a time. She feared the pain and mutilation of her body, but as long as it ended in long, permanent sleep, she would not protest or object. As Drabik drew near and poised the weapon at her tender loins, she cringed and closed her eyes, her body stiffening. She knew that despite her craving for an end to everything, she would scream and beg and plead for mercy, but she would hold out as long as she could.

Drabik's empty hand seized the girl's split nether lips and teased them. It was a pretty little cunt, he thought to himself. It wetted responsively, quickly. He fingered one of the little disks that hung there attached to a ring at the bottom of her labia. On it was a depiction of a mighty eagle, poised to strike, the emblem that Jake had selected as his own. It was the evidence of Jake's ownership of the slut. Well he would never see her again, that's for sure. Drabik brought the metal clipper adjacent to the girl's loins. He pushed it against her flesh.

The girl gave out a long, unhappy moan. Her whole body was trembling and shaking with dreadful fear at the prospective mutilation of her sexual organ. But Drabik had no intent on marring the pleasant flesh between his fingers. He grabbed the golden ring that pierced the girl's loins between the lips of the cutter and snapped it in two. He slid the ring through the little hole and tossed the broken ring and the disk to the floor. He then removed the other one. Reaching into his pants pocket her retrieved two identical little rings and disks. These disks contained a different crest. Not Jake's, not even Grobgy's, his lord and master.

These disks contained his own crest, the face of a snarling hyena. It was his first formal act in declaring his intent to found his own house, his own clan. The men who had done his preliminary dirty work on Klara were to be two of his loyal henchmen. Having satisfied their lusts on the brown haired girl, they surrounded him now. They watched as Drabik slid the opened rings through the holes in the girl's nether lips and clamped them closed with a pair of pliers. The open ends of the rings clicked into each other so that they could not be pried open again but would have to be removed with a heavy tool like he had done to Jake's rings. When the second ring was closed, the men shouted their approval and congratulations in Russian, shaking his hand and hugging him fiercely.

Klara felt the new rings being affixed to her body. So the man intended to let her live. But she would be his. This was God's punishment. She would have to bear this man's cruel depredations, service his flesh, endure his torments. Her face was a mask of agony as she looked into his hard, dark eyes.

"I am your new owner, Klara. Now, you belong to me." Drabik told her, confirming her fears. "You will find life with me a little different than life with your former owner. I detest you for your betrayal of your master and I intend to make the rest of your life as miserable as I can make it." His hand had delved between the moistened lips of her sex and was stroking her, exciting her against her will, even as a shroud of despair fell over her.

Klara could feel the man's thick fingers enter her and stroke the moist walls of her cleft. She whined when she sensed her blood beginning to rise. She was too well trained to avoid the consequences of the man's expert hand. Her whole body ached, the stripes where the whip had fallen burned. She could feel the throbbing of her still purple breasts. But none of that could dissipate the growing lust that she felt. She was a whore, she thought. She deserved all that happened to her. She was in the very hands of the devil himself and it was where she belonged. It had taken all of her life until now to learn her proper place. She groaned with unwanted pleasure as her pussy began to burn with desire.

She heard the tell tale sound of her new master's zipper being lowered. She felt its padded head seek its way between her hot nether lips made freely available by her split legs. She moaned when its thick length slid within her. She sighed deeply, "Ohhhhhhhhhhh!" when Drabik began to saw his ruthless prick back and forth deep inside.

Drabik groaned too when his piece slid home. The girl's hot, soft, wet walls of flesh clasped him tightly. His lusts had been growing ever since he had stepped into the room and the fact that he was demarking the beginning of his plot to make himself a lord and master of his own gang of hard, cruel men made the feel of the girl's helpless flesh exhilarating. He grabbed her hair at the back of her head and brought her lips to his. She gasped when she felt his thick, heavy tongue probe her mouth and groaned with pain as her tortured breasts were brought up against his chest. Her right leg, which was raised above her, rested against the man's left shoulder. Her new master, this dark, cruel sadistic demon, began to pump harder and harder against her.

And, in spite of her pain, in spite of her fear and hatred for this man who had had her torn from what was almost a paradise for her, Klara kissed him back madly, her own lusts beginning to boil over. When she felt his body stiffen, heard his deep, loud groan of pleasure, felt the splash of his hot cum inside her, she came as well. Torrents of hot passion flowed through her body. As the convulsions of her cunt came harder and harder, she screamed her pleasure into her master's mouth.

The killer slid his softening tool from the panting girl. He did not give her time to recover, but grabbed a thick plug gag from the table behind him and thrust it into her gasping mouth. He then took a black hood and covered her head with it.

"She's to be kept in this cellar at all times," he ordered his recruits. "There's a trap door in the last cell that leads to a lower level. Take her there. No one but one loyal to our endeavor is ever to see her. But you may all use her. She is the symbol of our undertaking. She is to be kept gagged and hooded at all times and beaten every day. Let anyone who betrays us know that their fate will be worse than hers."

The men acceded willingly to their new master's demands. No one crossed Anton Drabik. They had cast their lot with him, crossed the Rubicon. There was no going back, only success or death.

Drabik let the men have their will with his new property. He heard her cry out as he left the room, slamming the thick, steel door behind him. He had a lot to think about. He didn't know how he would use the limited knowledge he had gained tonight from the girl. What he had gleaned was that Jake, and probably Burnham, were engaged in a search for a girl named 'Maddy'. She was probably enslaved somewhere in Kalikastan and related to the one or both of them and maybe even a ponygirl. He couldn't tell whether they had found her or not. But he would. And he would find her first. If he could find out Burnham's game, get the girl they were looking for before they did, then he could blackmail Burnham for his support against Grobgy. He would get only one chance to overthrow the ganglord.

CHAPTER FIVE
A HARD LESSON FOR JAKE

Three men stood silently around a chair in the basement of the Burnham mansion. Sitting in the chair was the mangled, bloody form of what had once been a man. Blood had pooled around the chair and had thickened into a sticky, maroon mass as it had dried. Jake stared dolefully at the mess in front of him. To his right stood Tucker, one of his operatives, who had a similarly unhappy look, but one marked by elements of guilt and shame. To Jake's left stood the heavy set, black shirted form of Burnham's head of security, Nicholai Borodin.

It was Borodin who spoke first. "He was one tough motherfucker," he said admiringly. "We weren't able to get much out of him."

Jake looked at the security chief with disdain. Torturing this man to death was a convenient way of assuaging the blame for the theft of Jake's slave girl, Klara. The cow had already left the barn.

No single person but Borodin knew all of the security arrangements at the estate. Apparently, the man whose destroyed carcass was sitting in the chair, bound to it by black leather straps that criss-crossed his chest, had been unaware of the security cameras that caught his role in the abduction of the pretty, blond slave girl. Well, abduction was perhaps not the proper word. People were abducted and slave girls were not really people. Although closer to human than ponygirls, they were still considered to be a form of chattel. One didn't abduct chattel, you stole it.

In any case, the dead man had managed to disrupt the sweep of the main security cameras long enough so that his interaction with the slave girl had gone unrecorded. But redundancy was the key to security and he had been unaware of the other cameras that recorded the going ons of the estate from other locations. After he had been shown the video of him dumping the girl into the trunk of the Mercedes, he had ceased talking altogether and had said nothing else, other than screams and groans of pain, until he was dead. A large roll of Euro notes was found in his kit in the barracks, but nothing connecting him to any of the many criminal clans in the country.

Jake, however, did not need a roadmap to figure out who was involved. There was nothing so special about Klara that would have justified the time and effort that had been taken to steal her. She was pretty, yes, but so were many hundreds of other girls who lived lives of sexual bondage in this almost lawless country. In fact, the money found in the effects of the perpetrator would almost have been enough to purchase a good looking, if slightly used, slave girl outright. No, there had to be an underlying reason why somebody would go to so much trouble to kidnap his personal body slave. It had Drabik written all over it. Jake remembered their little tangle the night of the celebration of Lightning's championship. He had seen the deep mistrust and hatred in the ponygirl trainer's eyes.

Jake had gone thermonuclear when he had returned to the estate to find Klara missing. The night of Burnham's party he had enjoyed the pleasures of the slave girl Dana's body as well as that of the svelte red headed slave girl who had been assigned to his room. The newly enslaved and trained, young American girl had soft, pliant flesh. She demurely, but expertly, plied her lips over his swollen cock. After he had fucked her the first time, he recovered his forces while watching the redheaded slave delve between the American girl's thighs and bring her to several wrenching, noisy orgasms.

He was surprised the next morning when he ran into the caterer who was collecting his loaned out slave girls and supervising the breakdown of the catering equipment.

"You enjoy?" he asked Jake as he walked into the small dining room to get his well earned breakfast. The reference was obviously to the comely, black haired American slave girl Jake had used that night, a slave actually belonging to the portly restaurateur. Jake had gotten an exquisite good morning blow job from the red head while the American girl washed his body in the shower, and was reflecting on the pleasures of the Kalikastani way of life when the man approached him.

"Very much, thank you," Jake answered the man politely.

"She's yours," the man said, grinning.

"Mine?" Jake asked, astonished. "I don't get it."

"A gift from me to you," the man said.

"But I don't even know you," Jake said.

"But I know you, Mr. Barnes," the man replied. "You are a man of substance. We all expect great things from you. It is natural that a man of my status would want to, let us say, insure friendship."

Jake knew a bribe when he saw it. His first instinct was to refuse it. He already had a slave girl, one that, as luscious and lovely as she was, would be a hindrance when he finally was able to leave Kalikastan after his mission was complete. He didn't need another one. And an American at that. He had fucked American slave girls, yeah, but owning one would be crossing a line he preferred to leave uncrossed. Americans were supposed to help each other out when they were overseas, weren't they? Wasn't that the way it was in the movies? Not to mention being on the side of right and justice.

On the other hand, word that he had turned down a free slave girl, especially one of such delectable proportions and demeanor, would get around pretty quick. He was supposed to be a hard nosed slaver from America. If it got out what he was really up to he would be finished quickly. He accepted the bribe with apparent gratitude. He knew that eventually someone would come calling for a favor. By then, maybe, he'd be out of the country.

Later that morning, he led the unhappy, frightened, naked slave girl onto Burnham's huge traveling van and locked her into one of the four small cells. The driver brought in the former 'most beautiful girl in Croatia', Burnham's gift from the night before, and locked her into the cell next to Dana. The tall, lanky, beauty peered out of her tiny prison forlornly. There were traces on her skin of a mild whipping, probably required to insure her enthusiasm while being raped by Jake's boss last night after the party. Burnham was sure to have wanted to sample his gift right away.

Jake learned later that the girl had met the National Commission President, Kasparov, during his visit to Belgrade about a week ago. His money, handsome good looks, urbanity and powerful demeanor had swept the young model off her feet. They had partied for the week and she had accepted his invitation to visit his country. Her visit would be lasting much longer than she thought. Undoubtedly documents had been forged to show her exit from Kalikastan and disappearance in some foreign jurisdiction. Kasparov's people would have made sure that no one back in her home country would spend too much time looking for her.

The shapely, young woman was wearing a slave gag obscuring the lower portion of her face and her wrists were fastened behind her back by a newly acquired set of slave bracelets. When she got to Burnham's estate she could anticipate having her smooth, firm belly, one that she had undoubtedly strived mightily to keep lean and attractive, marred by a tattoo of Burnham's attack dog crest, her nether lips shaved and tagged and her new name etched over her soft, desirable breasts. While the Croatian girl peered at him intently, perhaps in the mistaken impression that he would do something to help her, Dana, his new property, knelt dejectedly in her small steel prison, her head hung low. Her existence as a commodity had just been dramatically reinforced. She was property to be kept or sold or given away at the whim of her owner. No one took the time to explain anything to her. Slave girls had no need of such knowledge.

They made a stop at Khalid's slave center before leaving Dlitski. Jake remembered it from when he first arrived in the country. They drove through the entrance into a large, cobblestone courtyard surrounded by two story barracks-like buildings. Khalid welcomed Burnham and Jake effusively. To call Khalid portly would be generous, as his belly was as round as a moon. His face was bearded and he had a wide, greasy grin. He disdained western clothing and wore a huge, multicolored, striped caftan. He offered Jake, Burnham and their security guard driver the use of the newly delivered girls who were lined up, standing naked and gagged on one side of the courtyard and contemplating their unhappy future. They were, according to Khalid, Romanian, and they uniformly had dark, tawny skin bespeaking, perhaps, gypsy heritage, and long, coal black hair. They would have been just removed from their shipping tubes and were probably no more than a week to ten days from their date of capture. It was a brave new world they were seeing for the first time, far from boyfriends, lovers, girlfriends and parents. Although they were gagged, their fear and apprehension was clearly evident on their faces through the widening of their eyes and the furrows in their brows.

They were all shapely and nubile, but Burnham demurred the courtesy and indicated that he would be pleased to look them over and any other girls Khalid might have on hand over for possible purchase. Khalid did most of the importing of new slave stock into Kalikastan and was a trusted, honest, dealer of flesh. Burnham had a side deal going with him in which he bartered some of the American girls that he sent the slaver from the States for girls of various other nationalities. Unbeknownst to Jake, Burnham was in the process of setting up expanded operations in the States, despite Mary Ellen's refusal to cooperate, and extending the reach of his acquisitions to Canada and Latin America. There were still some quirks to work out.

Burnham picked two from that lot: a diminutive lass with a saucy look to her eyes and long, flat hair that reached to her ass, and a taller girl of medium build with a long, narrow face and large breasts. Two more girls, a Dane and a German girl were selected from the general stock inside the barracks buildings. Burnham was finicky and he insisted on hands on sampling of over a dozen of the newly enslaved girls before making his selections. Once he had finished, Khalid had them loaded into the van and locked in cages. Since there were only four cages, the new girls had to double up. They squealed and protested behind their gags as their flesh was pressed into the steel enclosures. Jake's slave, Dana, knew enough already about how callously slave girls were treated and so gave no reaction as she watched the new girls being manhandled. But the

Croatian girl looked on with horror as she saw them crushed against each other's flesh, barely able to move. It would be extremely uncomfortable, and was certainly demeaning and callous, but it would only be for about nine hours or so while the van made its way back deep into the Kalikastani hinterland to Burnham's estate. They would suffer much worse when they got there.

Just before Jake got back into the van to leave, he heard a whistle blow and the door to one of the buildings opened. He had watched this spectacle before, but was mesmerized nonetheless as twenty-five or so naked slave girls, gagged and with their hands tied behind them, came pouring out of the building. They made a quick transit around the courtyard, huffing and puffing as they ran. Breasts bobbed to and fro and hair waved behind them as the girls, running as fast as their bare feet could take them, were harried on their rounds by two men with lashes,.

Although they were clearly distressed at the forced exercise, the wide eyed, huffing and puffing, new slave girls made their rounds silently except for the occasional whimper or moan when a lash struck skin. The exercise served several purposes. First, it prevented the girls from becoming too torporous in their long confinement in their stalls. Long hours sitting naked and gagged in their open doored stalls chained to the wall was depressingly boring, especially when the young girls naturally had so much on their minds. It also started the conditioning process whereby the girls would be trimmed down to delectable, lean and curvaceous figures, not that they weren't in pretty good shape already. The exercise also began to acclimate them to obeying the commands of masters, no matter how absurd or demeaning. And, finally, it was fun to watch: pretty, naked, young girls, mature in all physical respects, teary eyed and frightened, running desperately to please their masters.

When they arrived at the estate, Burnham's new sluts, including the unfortunate Croatian, were led off into the bowels of Burnham's mansion to begin their training. The new building, designed specifically for slave training purposes, was not yet complete. But it was almost done and would increase the training capacity of the estate significantly.

Jake towed his new acquisition, the unhappy Dana, over to the carriage house by a leash affixed to her collar, her face still gagged and her hands bound behind her. When he entered the kitchen, Tucker and Martinez were sitting morosely at the table. He knew as soon as he saw them that something was up. His heart sank as he saw all of their plans for rescuing Maddy go up in smoke. But it wasn't about Maddy, at least not directly. Tucker was the one who told him. Klara was gone. To Jake, she was not just a fucktoy. She was a woman who had touched something inside him. He had been worried for months about how he was going to live with himself if he abandoned her here, or, alternatively if he could manage her escape, what he would do with her then.

Tucker and Martinez hung their heads in shame as Jake took the kitchen apart. He smashed the table up against the wall, broke all of the dishes, shattered the windows with a chair and ranted and raved about their stupid incompetence. At one point, he pulled his pistol and held it aimed at his men, his arm and hand shaking in fury. The naked, gagged and bound American slave girl looked on in horror. What kind of man had she been given to? She started to cry.

When he had calmed himself back into a reasonable approximation of humanity, he barked at Martinez to,

"Lock this slut up in my room and keep her there! That is if you think you can do that without fucking it up!" The men had told him that the culprit was in Borodin's hands and Jake made a beeline for the mansion, the unhappy Tucker trailing forlornly behind him. He contained his rage as Borodin described his investigation and led him down into the basement to view the lifeless body of the criminal. After viewing the bloodied, ruined body of the man, Jake went up to Burnham's office. His fists still clenched and his blood still boiling, Jake approached the heavy oak doors that led to Burnham's large office. His 'secretary, "Betty', sat outside the doors and Jake asked her to announce him to the boss.

Betty was actually Burnham's former secretary from back in New York. He had enticed her over to Kalikastan, saying that he needed her for a few months. She did not know, of course, about the quaint customs of the former Soviet Republic. When she arrived, Burnham revealed to her that he knew that she had been stealing documents and records for purposes of blackmailing him some day. He had forced her to strip at gunpoint and then had raped her on his desk in front of Jake and a couple of his guards. She was then sent down below for some training in her new duties and he had given her the new name of 'Betty'.

Betty was older than the standard subject for enslavement in Kalikastan, having crested forty. But she was still a desirable, well kept female. She had large breasts that Burnham had been dying to see naked someday. They were full and firm even though they showed some evidence of her advancing years. Her body was trim, almost athletic and she had wavy chestnut hair.

Although Betty wore the tattoos customary for one of Burnham's slave girls, the angry, red eyed hound's head, her name stenciled above her breasts, Burnham had deviated from the norm in dictating her habiliment. Her name was written in deep blue, two inch high letters on her chest, but in English, rather than in the typical Cyrillic letters. He had had her head completely shaved, even to her eyebrows. She wore a large, golden ring through her nose, a decoration usually reserved for ponygirls, and he had rings with little bells attached set into her breasts, just above their downward arc, beneath her nipples. This left the nipples free for unobstructed oral stimulation. Her ears were pierced and little bells hung from rings in her earlobes. And where it was customary to shave clean the pudenda of slave girls, Burnham had arranged for Betty to keep her womanly growth. It was a heavy, curly, brown bush that, when left untrimmed, climbed up into the crease of her thighs and reached within inches of her waistline. It gave her, when contrasted with her otherwise hairless body, a strange, almost feral look. It emphasized her otherwise total nakedness in a way that denuded loins did not.

Burnham had a small, narrow table desk for her outside his office. It had no front and when one approached, you could see her widespread thighs and the hairy bush between them easily. Rather than a gag, Betty wore a large, round plug in her mouth that filled her oral cavity and distended her mouth. It had a small, plastic handle embedded in it that stuck out between her lips. Whenever anyone approached the office for the purposes of speaking to Burnham, she would pull the plug out, announce him over the intercom and then reinstall it once Burnham's answer was given.

Jake had a slight pang of conscience when he saw her as he stepped up the stairs that led to Burnham's office. He had met her several times in New York and had often admired her enticing cleavage in her low cut sweater or blouse. She was a strikingly handsome woman with fine features and smooth, tan skin. He had fucked her once since her enslavement, at Burnham's invitation. She had looked at him forlornly as he undressed and cried the whole time. Her little bells had tinkled musically as he had mounted from behind her while she was on all fours. But he had treated her tenderly and made her come three times. She had thanked him.

"Oh, Jake," she had whispered, "please help me, please. I can't take it here, please." The tears welled up in her eyes, strikingly piteous in the midst of her strange, bald head.

"Liz," he had answered her, his voice a mild remonstrance, stroking her cheek softly with his hand. "You know I can't do anything. He's in charge here. If there was anything I could do for you, I would," he said, the lie slipping easily over his tongue. Liz was not his problem. Jake was no knight in shining armor.

The former Elizabeth Crawly nodded forlornly. "I'm going to kill him," she said. "Somehow, I'm going to make him pay for this."

Jake rubbed her bald head and held her to him. "This will work out, Liz, I promise. Don't do anything foolish." A dead Burnham was the last thing he needed.

The unhappy woman nodded her head dolefully, her bells at her ears chiming softly. "Thank you, Jake," she said. "And please, come see me again. These other men…." He voice trailed off. Jake could just imagine what life in the Burnham mansion must be like.

On this day, as Jake rose on the stairs and his view moved up from the former secretary's bushy thatch between her thighs, he noted that Burnham had added something new, something which had turned the pleasant featured, sophisticated woman into something else entirely. Her head, face, shoulders, arms and breasts were covered with fresh yellow, green and red tattoos, each one finely surrounded by a serrated edge of blue. They were etched into her skin in a manner suggesting feathers, one row of colorful designs overlapping the other. On her upper body, only the flesh around the tips of her breasts had been left clear, a one inch wide swath of pale, white flesh around her nipples, which made the dark maroon areola stand out. Her name, 'Betty', etched into her skin above her breasts in bright, blue ink, was complemented by the bright, multicolored, lively designs that surrounded it.

When she saw Jake, her face cringed in shame. The large, round ball in her mouth made her cheeks bulge out. The leather bracelets on her wrists were connected by a chain that ran through the ring on her collar. It was long enough so that her hands could rest on the desk in front of her. Another chain, golden like the thick ring through her nose, to which it was attached, was connected to a ring embedded in the desk in front of her. She might spend many hours alone out here in the hallway, but she wasn't going anywhere without permission. The keys to her locks hung on the wall behind her out of reach.

Betty's upper body was in stark contrast to the clear skin of her naked legs and feet. It was like looking at some strange, alien creature, a humanoid bird of some sort, a figure from Hieronymus Bosch. Not the woman he had known in New York at all. Burnham was making her pay cruelly for her betrayal of him.

She pulled the plug from her mouth and started to say something to him, her eyes moistening. He silenced her with a wag of his finger. There was no sense her doing anything that would bring down the ire of her master. She pushed the intercom button. "Yes," Burnham's voice responded.

"Mr. Barnes to see you, Mr. Burnham," she said timidly. Burnham had apparently had her whipped recently as she bore bright, red stripes across her mature, full bosom, marks that melded nicely with the multicolored tattoos.

"Send him in," Burnham growled back.

Betty nodded to Jake and mournfully replaced the large, red rubber ball in her mouth, stretching her lips widely to receive it.

Burnham was sitting behind his huge, mahogany desk. He was alone but for a lanky, young, blond slave kneeling next to his desk. "Jake," he said as he rose from the desk, "I've heard all about it. I'm very sorry."

"I don't want you to be sorry, Mr. Burnham," Jake answered sternly. "I want you to do something about it!"

Burnham was pouring Jake a drink, a lowball full of ice and gin. "Here, have a drink, Jake," he said soothingly.

"I don't want a drink either, Mr. Burnham. I want my girl back and I want the people who took her to pay."

Burnham put the drink down on the desk and sat back next to it. Jake was standing about two feet away from him, his face a mask of rage. Burnham let him stew for a minute before answering him softly.

"Now, Jake, we don't even know who took her. It could have been anyone."

"You know who did it!" Jake retorted.

"And who is that?" Burnham asked, his voice now annoyed.

"Drabik, that's who!" Jake shouted. "You know that as well as me!"

"I don't know any such thing, Jake," Burnham replied hotly. "And neither do you. It could have been anybody." The sound of his own voice was approaching the ire in Jake's.

"That's bullshit!" Jake yelled. The two men stared at each other fiercely. Slowly, Jake began to recover his senses. He remembered who he was talking to: a man who had embraced the savagery of female slavery with abandon. He had his own agenda and was used to having his way. He could expect nothing from Burnham. If he crossed him, Burnham could order him out of the country or even have him killed. The tension in the room was acute as the men peered into each other's steely eyes.

"Okay, okay," Burnham said finally, looking away as he spoke. He walked over to the serving table and poured himself a scotch over ice. He took a long swallow. He was doing his own calculations. Jake was not a guy to fuck with. Sure, he had a phalanx of security guards, but if Jake wanted to, he could kill him with a single blow before he reached the phone. And he needed him. He needed his loyalty. After all, if the powers that be decided that Burnham was no longer useful to them, he would be in deep shit. Only Jake could protect him. And there was the Maddy thing. He hadn't forgotten about that. And, he was sure, neither had Jake. He would play the Maddy card.

"Listen, Jake," he told him calmly, "have you forgotten why we're here? I haven't. And you shouldn't either. I hired you because you're the best. You always get the job done. And I'm counting on you to do it." His voice turned more intense, more purposeful now.

"I don't know who stole your whore and, frankly, I don't care. You belong to me until this job is done and you can't let anything personal get in the way. I can't help it if you foolishly let yourself get hooked into one of these sluts. You should have known better."

Jake was standing before the billionaire, inwardly seething, but knowing that every word that he said was true.

Burnham continued. "There's about thirty five slave girls on this estate alone who would bend their bodies in half at your slightest desire. They'll fuck you, suck you, smile, swallow your spunk, take it up the ass, do anything you want and never complain. And you thought that this one was something special? Maybe she was, but I could get a dozen more special sluts here tomorrow. You can take your pick. So get off of it Jake. What were you going to do with her anyway when the job is done? Take her with you?"

And there Burnham had him. What would he have done with her anyway? He remembered her soft smile and comely eyes. He could only hope that they were shining for someone else now and that she wasn't lying dead somewhere on the Kalikastani plains. Her time had come, that's all. It would have happened sooner or later. At least this way he didn't have to watch her go. But still, he thought, there had been something. She had belonged to him and he had protected her. He was no fool. Maybe now she was gone. Maybe it was better this way. But Drabik would pay. That was one thing he promised himself.

"Okay, Mr. Burnham," he told his boss. "I get your point. But when all this is done, I'm going to take care of my business. And you better not get in my way. Got it?"

Burnham smiled. All was well in paradise. "I get it Jake," he responded. "Now we have to talk practicalities." He looked at the slave girl who was kneeling by the desk. Klara's kidnapping had highlighted to him at least a gap in security. Slave girls could talk. And they could listen. He wasn't going to take any more chances. "Get the fuck out of here," he said to her gruffly. "Wait outside."

The pretty, lean, blond girl rose to her feet hurriedly. Her slave disks between her legs tinkled as she scurried from the room. When the door shut behind the obedient girl, Burnham sat back in his chair behind his carrier sized desk. It supported only a widescreen laptop computer, a neat, Kelly green desk pad, the intercom and a small pile of papers. There was also a small black telephone, restricted to local use only. It would not do for a slave girl to be able to pick up a phone and call home. All international calls were made by specially licensed cell phones. Possession of an unlicensed one was a capital offense. Burnham's was the only one on the estate. He communicated with his New York office by a special computer link.

"Okay, Jake, let's assume that Drabik took the girl. Is he likely to get anything out of her, anything about Maddy?" This, for Burnham was the real crux of the problem.

Jake thought carefully before answering. He converted himself to his deadly, business mode, all emotions repressed. "Well, she didn't speak much English," he said slowly, realizing as he did that he was speaking of the lovely slave girl in the past tense. "And we don't go gabbing about what we're working on. She might have picked up a word or two. Maybe the name 'Maddy', but, unless Drabik knows specifically what to look for, that won't do him any good. He knows her only as 'Lightning'. As far as I know, Khalid won't have any records of her pre-ponygirl name."

Burnham looked at Jake seriously. "I hope you're right, Jake. It'd be a shame if we lost Maddy after all of this trouble. Not to mention our sweet set up here."

"You mean your sweet set up, Mr. Burnham. I'm just here for the job."

"Sure, Jake, sure. And when it's all over your going to go back to the world and forget about how you could get laid five times a day by the most willing, beautiful females that could be found."

Jake pondered the barb that his boss had thrown at him. He looked at the empty bank of slave cages behind Burnham's desk, the pile of chains and slave bracelets in the corner of the room, the array of whips on the walls.

"Willing?" Jake asked, sarcastically. "Did you say 'willing'?

"Don't give me this crap, Jake. Did you ask Betty for permission to fuck her two weeks ago? Did your slut, Klara beg you to fuck her up the ass? And the setup you took over in New Jersey for me, are the girls banging on the doors pleading to be sent overseas to be whipped and raped and beaten by as many men as possible? Get off of it!"

"But deep down, you know it's wrong, Mr. Burnham. And so do I."

"Listen, Jake, little people don't matter. They never have. All through history, millions, billions of people have been exploited, murdered, slaughtered, enslaved, all in the name of empire or religion or power or nationality. When the US bombs a village in Afghanistan or Iraq, does it beat itself over the head because 'innocent' women and children have been killed? Does any government? And when the government can draft men and send them to slaughter in the name of General Motors, oil, 'the reputation of the United States' does anyone question their right to use of those young lives?"

Jake was wordless. He knew that Burnham would never be convinced by any argument he had. Who knows, maybe he was right. But it all came down to what you chose as an individual, didn't it? Didn't it? But he had never lived that way. He had killed 'innocent' people. Witnesses, by-standers, people who had become dangerous to others by what they knew. What difference did it make if you killed one innocent person or enslaved thousands?

A cold stream of self hate flowed across Jake's breast. He had never asked these questions before. He should forget them now. He looked at Burnham. He wasn't really expecting an answer, was he?

"Let's get down to business, Jake," he said, leaning back in his large, brown leather chair. "I understand that your girl, Chocolate, is coming along nicely."

"I wouldn't know, Mr. Burnham," Jake answered dully. "I've kept myself away from the track so she wouldn't see me."

"Well, in a few minutes I'm having a meeting of the racing staff," Burnham continued. "The fall season's a little over two weeks away. We'll be handing the ponies over to the drivers tomorrow morning. I want your input."

"I don't know anything about ponygirl racing, Mr. Burnham," Jake answered.

"But you know people, Jake," Burnham retorted. "And that's why I want you there. I want to know who's lying."

* * * * * * * * * * * * * *

At two o'clock, fifteen men sat in Burnham's cavernous living room awaiting the arrival of the 'chief'. Jake sat on one of the sofas that had been arranged in a 'U', all facing a large, brown easy chair where Burnham would sit when he arrived. There was a long table filled with post conference treats and several slave girls were serving drinks and appetizers to the men. They were a rough looking bunch, men used to handling human females in the cruelest, most callous manner possible. Jake doubted that they had any qualms about what they did.

Betty was prominent among the serving girls. Jake watched them cast fearful, sideways glances at her, shocked by the monster that she had become. For all the other girls knew, it would be what all the slave girls would be wearing soon. Most of them probably believed that they would be free one day. A lifetime of slavery was too much for the civilized Western mind to contemplate. Somebody would rescue them. A master would fall in love with them and free them. Something. But who would want them if they were all marked up like that?

The former secretary's appearance was more bird like when she stood. Her wrists were still bound by a chain through her collar and her bent elbows looked like little wings. Her face was round and distorted by the large ball that she kept inserted in her mouth. And her naked, pale legs with the rampant brown bush between them looked like little bird's legs. Due to the confinement on her wrists, she had to bend over to pour a drink and when she did, she looked like some huge, tropical, avian creature bobbing for insects. She looked at Jake ruefully while she poured him lemonade from a large pitcher. Her breasts swayed as she leaned over and the unmarked, pale circles of flesh around her areola dangled invitingly before him. He wondered what it would be like to fuck her now.

Burnham entered the room and everyone sat up at attention. He was wearing one of his standard Izod shirts and a pair of tan slacks over black, Italian shoes. He sat in his chair and Betty came over to offer him some lemonade. He held out his glass with one hand and tinkled the little bell beneath her left breast with the other. "Good afternoon, Betty," he said. "Thank you for the lemonade. Perhaps we should have a little session together later. Would that be nice?"

The secretary visibly shivered at her owner's suggestion and spilled a small drop of lemonade on the rug. She stood back in horror.

A dark cloud crossed over Burnham's face. "Get down and lick that up, cunt," he ordered menacingly. "I see that you are in need of another lesson in deportment." He put his glass down on the small table next to his chair. His birdlike secretary carefully placed the large glass pitcher she was holding down next to it and dropped to her knees. She bent her head down to the floor and began lapping up the spilled liquid. It had only been a drop, but the woman was careful to make a diligent effort, covering a wide circle on the rug with her tongue. Her appearance was that of a huge, colorful dodo bird digging for worms. When done, she looked up at her master nervously.

"Now go down to the barracks and find someone to give you ten strokes with the cane," Burnham ordered her. "Tell him that I want it on your ass and thighs so I can see the marks. Be back in twenty minutes or I'll whip you some more myself."

Betty nodded forlornly and rose to her feet. She gave an unhappy glance at Jake as she ran from the room, her bound hands dangling before her, her little bells jingling. Jake felt sorry for her, but he shrugged it off.

"Now," Burnham announced, "let's get down to business. How are we doing?"

The head trainer, a fortyish, hard looking man with a finely muscled body and short cut, brown hair started off. His name was Mitya Sokolov and he was somewhat young for his post. He had developed a fine reputation for the handling of ponygirls and Burnham had hired him away from his last employer based on his reputation. He was a harsh taskmaster and insisted on firm ponygirl discipline.

"You've recruited some fine stock, Mr. Burnham, and I believe that we will make a good showing for your first season. Itzak and Gavinski have done a great job with the six pony team and we should win a few races there. Don't forget, it takes at least a year for a team like that to really get into top form. It's a lot of weight to pull and they really need to work together for a long time. A few of them are new to their bits and it took some work to get them running properly. If I had anything to say about it though,

I'd look for another pair of leaders. The number one and two ponies are good, but not really championship material. They are the key ponies in that team and if you want the team to flourish, you've got to get the best."

Burnham looked over at Itzak and Gavinski, the trainers of the six pony team. That team pulled a large cabriolet carriage and two riders, one in the driver's seat bedecked in a footman's livery and another in the cab, dressed formally like a nineteenth century gentleman down to the top hat and tails. Although not considered by true aficionados as the cream of the sport, the crowds loved the cabriolet races for the pure spectacle. The carriage that they would pull at the actual races would be finely turned out with gold painted appointments, large, colorful banners and Burnham's crest on its doors.

"Well, let's hope they make a good showing at least," Burnham said to the trainers, somewhat irritated.

Mitya continued his presentation. "The yearlings are coming along fine. We had a good selection to pick from."

The yearling trainer was an older, mild looking man with balding grey hair and thick, wire rimmed glasses. His mild demeanor was deceptive. His charges had suffered greatly for their failings during training. "I had the six yearlings you bought worked out in all combinations," he told the boss. "I finally settled on the Norwegian blond and the red tailed Irish pony, Venus and Fireball. One of the others, Prancer, a Belgian, might be good for the cabriolet. She's strong and has quick legs."

Mitya nodded at the suggestion. "I'll have her work out with them. But don't count on anything from her this season, especially as a leader. I'll let her practice in the number three position and, if she has the stuff, I can move her up in the spring."

"Okay," said Burnham. "I'll have my people keep a look out for another good prospect. Jake," he said, looking at his fixer, "let our US contacts know what we're looking for. We have a huge pool of females to pick from in the States and there's no reason we can't pick up a couple of good prospects there."

Jake nodded dutifully. He would do no such thing. Once the fall season was over and Maddy was liberated, he was out.

The men discussed the other heats they would be contesting, the troika, and a four ponied post chaise. The nine pony landau, a large, classical carriage, would not be ready this season. Then the discussion came around to the 1500 meter sulky and Chocolate. Irkut spoke up.

"She's running real well." He pointed to the diminutive man sitting next to him. "Giorgi has looked her over and he thinks that he can shave another ten or twenty seconds off of her time with a little encouragement. That should make her a real contender."

Giorgi was one of the Gromyko brothers, twin dwarfs who specialized in driving ponies in the sulky races. They were well known as cruel, almost vicious drivers and their ponies were maintained under the most harsh conditions during the racing season. They were both eminently successful. His brother Jerzi had driven Lightning to the championship in the spring. He was a cinch to be handling her again this fall. Burnham was hoping to pit the brothers against each other in the fall championship. If Chocolate could gain the final against Lightning, then he would challenge Grobgy to make it a claiming race. It was the type of bet the gangster would find it impossible to resist.

Giorgi had driven the 3000 meter sulky for the Grobgy estate the year before and had finished second in the tournament. His pony had suffered appropriately for her loss. He had a number of championships under his belt, six compared to his brother's ten. Jerzi was generally considered the better of the two but he already had a champion ponygirl to drive, Lightning. Burnham had hired Giorgi as soon as the scheme to set Jackie, now Chocolate, against Maddy, now Lightning, had been put in place.

Jake shuddered for the young, black whore he had recruited. He had heard tales of Giorgi's cruelties. If Jackie thought that she had it hard now, she had another thing coming. The racing season lasted about ten weeks. Other ponies had suffered through Giorgi's brand of hell and survived. Jackie would too, although he could not vouch what damage it might do to her long term. But a million dollars could buy a lot of psychotherapy.

Betty had returned during the conference and she was standing by the door awaiting orders. Fresh, bright red wounds, certain to turn black and blue, covered the front of her thighs. Her eyes were red rimmed. Burnham motioned her to come over to him and he ordered her to turn around so that he could see her rear. Five red lines ran across her buttocks and the tops of the back of her thighs. He smiled at her approvingly and then tumbled her over his lap. His hand captured her hairy loins and he began to toy with her sex.

The conference lasted another ten minutes or so and by the end, Betty's sex was leaking fluids and the bird woman was moaning quietly. He pushed her off of his lap and stood. "Thank you, gentlemen. I know you will all do your best. And now, please enjoy my hospitality." He swung his hand in a wide gesture indicating the long table full of exquisitely prepared dishes. The men gave various grunts of approval and began to sidle up to the chow.

Betty had regained her feet and Burnham snapped a leash onto the golden ring in her nose. He signaled his farewell and led the colorful creature from the room. Jake wasn't hungry but he was interested in speaking to Irkut. Irkut knew that Jake had 'recruited' Chocolate, and knew of the plans to challenge Lightning to a claiming race. Hopefully, he had not guessed at the personal interest that Jake and Burnham had in its outcome. Several of the men already had slave girls servicing them, either on their knees, their pretty, well trained lips around their cocks, or upended over a sofa, plowing them from behind. Irkut was eating a plateful of well seasoned veal and fresh, crisp vegetables. Giorgi was next to him. He had chosen some of the grilled salmon.

"Do you really think that Chocolate has a chance?" Jake asked the trainer.

It was Giorgi who replied. "I wouldn't be here if she didn't." He had a neatly trimmed, black beard that circumscribed his broad, little chin. His hands looked strong and large for his body. Size mattered in the sulky races and there was no minimum weight limit. So the estates recruited the smallest, strongest men that could be found as drivers. The smaller and lighter they were, the less drag on the ponies. And they needed their strength to enforce their will on the former human females.

He looked up at Jake. "I hear you picked her out. Is that true?"

"I knew of her in Chicago. She had run track a few years ago and had been pretty good," Jake answered him.

Giorgi laughed. "You have to be a cold hearted bastard to recruit someone you know to be a ponygirl. I admire that."

Jake bristled at the description of himself, but decided to let it go. After all, it was true.

The dwarf continued. "After tomorrow, that pony's life will be hell. I didn't come here to finish second." He was chewing on his fish as he spoke. "Fear is the great motivator for ponygirls," he continued, "and the one that has the most to fear from losing is the one that usually wins. She'll rue the date of her birth if she fucks up on me."

Giorgi's voice, deep and gravelly, was matter of fact. He obviously meant what he said and was not given to hyperbole. Jake shuddered for the brown skinned whore.

After the meal, Jake took a long walk around the grounds of the estate. It was a busy place. Construction was going on in the new training facility and the sound of drills and hammers filled the late afternoon air. He paused at the ponygirl track and watched some of the ponies being taken through their paces. He was careful to watch out for Jackie since he had been told that her seeing him might interfere with her training. As a pair of young, sprightly ponygirls zipped past, pulling behind them the yearling ponygirl cart, he wondered how their minds coped with their newly dehumanized states. He watched as they rounded the track at full speed. This was Venus and Fireball, the ones that had been spoken of. He had bought them both on Burnham's behalf last spring and he remembered their fearful skittishness as he had tested the firmness of their flesh, probed their hairless loins. It had all been for show, of course. Irkut was the expert.

As the pretty, naked yearlings approached him from the home turn, he admired their bounteous breasts as they recorded each determined stride. His loins stirred. He heard the crack of the whip on their backs as they passed him and headed for the finish line. Was Burnham right? Was this a sweet setup? The six pony team rumbled past next, their combined hoof beats, all in strict unison, creating a rumble in the dirt. So many, he thought. So many women taken from their lives. All for what?

He left the track and walked down past the work ponygirl barn where he saw Tucker hitching up Dora and Flora. The two tall, broad shouldered ponies stood obediently still as he applied their leather straps. Jake stopped and watched silently as Tucker eased them back into the traces of the two pony cart and affixed the long, wooden shafts that led from the cart to their right and left hips.

Jake had learned that these females had been ponies for over seven years, most of that on the same racing team. He wondered if there was any humanity left in them at all. Their lips were pulled back by their cruel bits in identical macabre grimaces. They looked almost like twins, the black neoprene hoods concealing all identity. It was doubtful that they had even ever seen each other's faces. The pony pair wore tattoos of a green, red and yellow snarling tiger on their bellies and their names stenciled over their breasts in 2" high blue, Cyrillic letters. Long, yellow ponytails emerged from their hoods and descended their backs. Jake stepped forward to examine them more closely and softly caressed Dora's left breast. It was large and firm and conveyed the warmth of her body to his hand. The pony didn't react to his handling of her except that the nipple stiffened obediently when he drew his thumb across it.

Tucker finally decided that he would break the silence between himself and his boss.

"Jake, I'm really sorry about Klara. I fucked up. I can't tell you how bad that makes me feel."

It was the most personal information that the tall, broad shouldered, hard man had ever communicated to Jake. Jake just looked at him, his unhappiness clear in his face. He was trying to empty his mind of all thoughts of what the slave girl had probably suffered as a result of her kidnapping. She would have been subjected to the cruelest treatment that these extraordinarily cruel people could devise. He wondered if she was still alive. Once they had beaten all of the information out of her that they could, she would be of little use except as an advertisement of Drabik's crime against him.

Tucker had the strong, blond haired ponies fully hitched now to the cart. He handed Jake the reins. "Take them out for a ride, Jake, it'll do you some good. Burnham sent down word that he'd be busy this afternoon. They know the way. Just give them a little snap of the reins and they'll take you for a nice five mile ride."

The thought of getting away from the estate proper for a while pleased Jake and he thanked Tucker for the offer. He had driven the team once or twice, but only over short distances. He climbed up in front of the cart and took a seat. He flicked the reins once and the ponies sprang to life.

The heavy black boots produced a pony-like clip clop as the cart was pulled out onto the macadam pathway. It took a few moments for Jake to get comfortable, but he soon was leaning back on the wooden seat and enjoying the soft breeze as the cart picked up a little speed. The ponies trotted in finely tuned unison, their haunches flexing and softening on each stride of their strong legs. Their ponytails bounced gracefully behind them. The leather traces that led to their harnesses were pulled taut, but the leads to their bits, which sat in Jake's hands, remained loose. There was no real need to drive these ponies, Tucker was right. Pulling a cart was their life and they were an expert team.

A fine sheen of sweat started to arise on their backs as they gracefully pulled the cart along. The estate was set within a basin surrounded by meandering hills and the ponies crested these with ease. The well groomed lawns of Burnham's estate gave way to tall, yellow and green, wide bladed grass. The sky was a deep blue with nary a cloud and the August sun beat down on the ponies and Jake. He drew off his dark blue polo shirt and tossed it back in the cart. He was wearing a pair of faded, light blue jeans and black, ankle height athletic shoes. He decided to let the ponies run a little bit and he gave the reins a flip. Immediately, the pair of well trained ponies shifted gear and increased their pace.

The road dipped down into a small glen and then entered a forest. The trees were tall and lush with bright green leaves. It was peaceful and quiet except for the clatter of the ponies' hoofs on the hard road. The road passed over a small brook and the sound of the heavy black boots of the ponies echoed on the little wooden bridge. Jake felt some of the anger and pain ease out of him. He reached into his pants pocket and pulled out a pack of Lucky's. He held the reins in one hand while he snapped his lighter open and, after firing up the tobacco, took a long, satisfied, deep drag.

Jake's body welcomed the familiar reaction to the nicotine. The woods were dark, the trees over hanging the narrow track, and it had cooled. But the coolness was refreshing and Jake had no need to redon his shirt. He smiled as he thought of himself as on an exotic amusement park ride, everything around him having been planted and maintained for his delight. A pair of large, broad winged, black birds flitted across the road, their screeching piercing the otherwise silent forest. Here and there squirrels raced along the trees' extended branches.

The trail meandered gently through the forest. When the path began to edge along a large lake, Jake eased back on the reins to slow the ponies down. Light glimmered off of the lake's smooth surface. He decided to stop the cart so that he could enjoy the view. He gently urged the ponies to a halt and, after tying off the reins to the cart, jumped down. He took a look in the back of the cart and found a hamper with some cheeses and sausages in it along with a bottle of deep red wine. Apparently the cart had been stocked for Burnham's comfort. Jake decided that he would avail himself of Burnham's picnic and brought the hamper over to a wide, grassy area near the lake. Looking back, he decided to let the ponies free from their traces for the time being rather then making them stand and await his leisure.

The ponies were still breathing heavily when he approached them. Their chests were not straining, they were in excellent shape, but the results of their workout were evident. Jake paused to admire the rising and falling of their plump, pale white orbs and their sweaty, naked nether lips. His hands explored their heaving breasts and then drew over their firm, colorful bellies. He took possession of both of their naked, hairless slits at the same time and he sensed their accommodation to his caresses as their bodies relaxed and their thighs spread. Soon, their pussies were moist and loose and, when he teased their hardened pleasure nubbins at the apex of their tender, hot slits, they both sighed as if in unison.

Jake's cock had grown hard and his desire was on him. He looked at the widespread mouths of the two ponies and tried to decide which pair of lips he would use to bring himself to completion. Flora, the pony to his right, gave a deep moan of pleasure and he decided to choose her. Freeing his hands from the ponies' quims, he unhooked Flora's hips from the shafts of the cart and undid the reins from her bit. The pony's breasts had become hard and swollen at her developing lust and Jake took one of her thick nipples in his lips. His mind swooned at the taste of her sweaty flesh and the sensation of her firm bud in his mouth. He caressed and kissed both breasts until he brought another moan from the former human female. He then placed his hands on her shoulders and lowered her to her knees.

Both Flora and Dora were a few inches taller than him and Flora's mouth came to just above his waist. He reached behind her head and unfastened the harsh steel bit that distended her lips and eased it out. Flora opened her mouth expectantly. Jake freed his hardened manhood from his jeans and presented its, plump, soft helmet to her lips. He eased it slowly into her mouth, sighing as he savored her moist warmth.

The pony's able tongue swirled over Jake's cock sending a wave of pleasure through him. His knees sagged and he placed his hands on her strong shoulders for support. The black hooded head drew back slowly, dragging the pony's lips along his sensitive shaft, pausing momentarily as the underside of his cock's head breached her mouth's entrance. He felt her tongue tease the tiny opening and then the head moved slowly forwards, engulfing his manhood until the rigid pole pierced her esophagus.

Jake's mind swam with pleasure. He rocked himself gently to match the pony's rhythm. The sun beat down on his naked torso and a slight breeze wafted over him. He sensed the other pony, Dora, shift her feet nervously next to him and he took his left hand and recovered possession of her lush slice. She made a half whinny, half human sound as he buried his fingers within her. His hand began to match the strokes on his cock by Flora's mouth and he felt Dora's thighs spread and her hips begin to gently gyrate.

Slowly, surely, Jake's need began to rise within him. He pinched and tickled Dora's stiff clit to bring her along. Flora's efforts became more intense as she sensed his passions building to a crescendo. Jake moaned and arched his back as the sensations of the lips and hot tongue on his cock beclouded his mind. He held back as long as he could. He wanted Dora to come, to accentuate his own crisis. When he heard her heavy breath begin to shorten and intensify, little moans emerging from her throat, he let himself go. He groaned as the first powerful throb of his cock made all of the muscles of his body contract. He felt himself pouring out through his pulsing rod. Dora snorted and moaned as she came, her hips thrusting at his hand.

With a loud moan of pleasure, Jake shot the last of his creamy load into Flora's comforting, soft mouth. His body weak from his pleasure, he pulled his meat gently from between her lips and stepped back. He patted the anonymous, black hooded head tenderly in thanks for her efforts. After recovering his sensibility, he decided to free both of the ponies from the cart and let them cavort while he enjoyed the repast he had found. When they were both free of the traces, their harnesses still cinched around their torsos, he led them over to the wide expanse of soft grass that led up to the lake. He motioned for them to kneel as he sat. Their tiny eye holes seemed to peer at him expectantly. He knew what they wanted. He nodded his head and they turned to each other. He had released Dora's bit when he freed her from the cart and the two ponies' lips met.

Flora and Dora pressed their full, pillowy breasts against each other and reveled in each other's mouths. That the two ponies had a deep, desperate passion between them could be easily seen. Their black, neoprene covered heads parted slightly and Jake watched as their tongues tasted each other's lips, intertwined and then pressed hard against each other.

When the ponies rolled to their sides in the grass, Jake decided to join their nakedness. The plush, natural setting seemed inappropriate for dress and he shucked his shoes and jeans off quickly. While Dora and Flora twisted and turned their bodies together, kissing each other's breasts, licking at their bellies, Jake opened the bottle of deep red colored wine and took a long swig. He leaned back on his elbows and enjoyed the spectacle of the pale white ponies forming a two backed beast, their sexes rubbing, their mouths firmly clamped together.

The ponies pleasured each other for at least twenty five minutes. Flora buried her head between Dora's thighs and gave her long, languorous strokes with her accomplished tongue. Dora came for the second time, moaning her pleasure loudly. And then it was Flora's turn to writhe and moan under the lips of her cart mate. Jake nibbled at the cheese and took hard bites from the dried sausage that was in the hamper. He also drank about half a bottle of the wine as he relaxed in the quickening sun. As he began to nod off from the effects of the wine and his recent sexual release, his hand tightened on the long leather leashes he had attached to the rings in the ponies' collars when he released them from the cart. His right hand casually and absent mindedly stroked his loins, his cock rising to a lazy stiffness as his eyelids closed. As he drifted off to slumber, the ponies had turned their bodies and had their heads buried deeply between each other's thighs.

When Jake awoke, he felt a mouth gently caressing his stiffened cock. It took a moment for him to realize where he was. Automatically, he checked to see if the leashes to the ponies' collars was still in his hand. If they had run off, he would never in this lifetime be able to catch them. Although someone would eventually, Tucker would probably kill him first.

But the leads were still there. As he recovered his senses, he felt one of the ponies crawl next to him and leaning over, offer her heavy, soft breast to his lips. The softness of the breast that pressed against his lips overwhelmed him. He suckled at the stiff nipple hungrily. For a moment, he wondered at the ponies' sexual aggressiveness, but realized that it was probably their way of thanking him for their own private, intense sexual interlude. And it was getting late. They had let him sleep peacefully and then, when the shadows began to lengthen around the lake, had decided to waken him. They had a routine, after all, and when the sun began to fall, it was their time to return to the ponygirl barn, get their rubdowns and feed.

Jake could not tell which pony's breast was in his mouth and he didn't care. He pulled her torso towards him and seized her other breast with his lips. The mouth on his cock was tormenting him and he felt his balls tighten with the need for release.

The impassioned fixer grabbed the tail of the pony on top of him and drew her lips to his mouth. He thrust his hot tongue inside her. The rough leather of her harness pressed against him and her hard nipples and her soft breasts were crushed atop him. He felt like his body was being consumed by two hungry mouths as his cock began to ache with need. "Auurrrrrrrrrrrrgh!" he shouted from deep in his chest as his orgasm overcame him. "Aurrrrrrrgh! Aurrrrrrrrgh!" he called out, the almost painful pulses of pleasure tearing through him.

As his paroxysms of pleasure faded, the mouth on his cock softly milked his softening tool for its last drop of semen. His grip on the ponytail of the creature atop him loosened and the kisses between him and the obliging female slowed to languorous, post climax bliss. He tenderly pushed her aside and rose to his feet. It was Dora whose mouth had brought him to completion and he gave her another kiss before he slipped her steel bit back into her

mouth. When he had restored Flora's bit, he led the ponies
back to the cart. He tied off the leashes that went to their
collars to the cart and returned to the grassy scene of his
recent delight. He looked out at the vast expanse of the
lake. The sun was just turning a tint of orange and the
colors of the lake and its environs were transforming to
gentle pastels. His body was loose and relaxed. He felt
sluggish and satisfied but he needed to bring himself back
to full alertness. He was still naked and he ran into the lake
impetuously. It became deep almost immediately and he
dove down until he was completely immersed. The water
was cold, apparently being from an underground spring,
and his mind came crashing back to acuity. He swam about
twenty strokes towards the center of the lake and then
back. His long, hard strokes left him gasping for air as he
rose back onto the shore. He reveled in the coolness on his
body. He felt like his moroseness had deserted him, been
chased away by the physical and mental delights of this
long afternoon. Tucker had been right. This was just what
he needed. He dressed quickly and put the hamper and half
empty bottle of wine back in the cart. He rehitched the
ponies, caressing them softly in appreciation of the pleasure
that they had brought him. He then hopped back up onto
the driver's seat, gave the reins a little tug and Dora and
Flora jumped to life, wheeling him back to the estate and
reality.

CHAPTER SIX
THE END OF LOVE

The light, leisurely workouts of summer had turned into long and arduous repetitions of turns around the practice track. Lightning at first welcomed the return to serious training. She had felt her leg muscles turning soft and there had been a certain lack of purpose in her days. But now, her driver ran her until her legs felt that they would give way. After each prolonged session, she would be returned to the pony barn and given a comforting rub down. She was glad for the strong hands of the trainer along her back and thighs. The balm that he rubbed into her muscles burned and then soothed them.

Each day, she seemed to run a little longer. Her driver had taken to the use of the whip to encourage her, something that he hadn't needed to do before. Each time that her legs became too heavy to lift, she would feel the crack of the whip on her back and its intense sting. She hated the whip. Although she had come to terms with her life as a ponygirl, she had never fully given up her idea of herself as a woman, a person. The whip was a reminder of her bestiality in the eyes of the men who controlled her. She might think of herself as some kind of exotic athlete, but they thought of her as an animal, one who understood only the most elementary forms of communications.

And the whip reminded her of her total and complete loss of control of herself. A person might say 'stop', 'I need a rest,' or 'enough!'. However, not only did she not have the physical ability to speak, unless you could call the mangled sounds that she could make through her sharp and painful steel bit as words, but the men would have thought it odd that a beast would presume to tell them what to do with her. They would have laughed as they brought out the cane to drive into her flesh another lesson in subservience.

And she did see some of the other ponies caned, quite often. Ponies were being worked into teams, older, tired ponies were being weeded out. And the new ponies, the ones newly dehumanized, suffered the most, as she had when she was a yearling. Of course, Lightning did not know the term 'yearling', the pony racing name for ponies new to their bits. She almost never knew what the men were talking about since they always talked in Russian. She had learned maybe twenty or twenty five words in that strange language. Most had to do with the need for speed, such as, '*Nezoi! Nezoi!*', which meant that she should go faster. Or the words for 'open your mouth' so that a gag or a cock could be inserted.

She had learned the meaning of her Russian ponygirl name, '*Molnya*' or Lightning. It was a name that she, ironically, was proud to bear. She had long ago decided that if she was condemned to be raced like an animal, she would be the best that she could be. She wore hooked to her ponygirl collar a gold medallion that said that she was a champion. She had bested the best. They had taken her picture, her neck adorned with garlands, her owner, trainer and driver standing there with her for the sake of posterity. She had never been in the big mansion on the hill, but she imagined the picture in some place of pride in her owner's living room or office. (In fact, Grobgy had a wall in his office bedecked with photos of his numerous champions and Lightning's was there prominent among them.)

And there was another thing that gave her pause as she came to understand that another racing season was near. At some point, probably not too far away, she would be handed over to her racing driver, the dwarfish devil who had tormented and abused her unmercifully in the spring.

When she thought of that man, her blood ran cold. And she would be separated from the object of her abject adoration, the man who had first trained her, Drabik. She didn't know his name, but she dreamt of his scarred, harsh face and yearned for his rigid, demanding manhood. He would have no access to her during the racing season. And neither would any of the other men. And neither would Persephone, her ponygirl lover. She hadn't seen her since the interlude with Anya in the woods, but she hoped that her trainer would give her one last chance to kiss her lips and sink her tongue into the depths of her womb before racing season started.

Like the other ponies, she had become addicted to the habitual use of her body for the sexual amusement of the men. Each morning, she waited eagerly for the stable boy or a trainer to come to her stall and bring her to orgasmic completion. She bucked and heaved as the men used her pussy or ass throughout the day, and moaned and cried out behind her gag with relish as she achieved another mind wrenching orgasm. And she had come to cherish the feel of a hard cock in her mouth and throat, hearing the men moan and grunt with pleasure as she serviced them, beaming with pride as she received their discharge and felt their members throb within her. Her driver, Jerzi, used her sexual needs as a part of his control of her. He would taunt her sexually, bring her near to completion and no more, leave her gasping and moaning, rubbing her thighs together in frustration. When he used her mouth, he would pull back when he felt his seed begin to spill and jerk himself off into her mouth as if disdainful of her skills. Last spring she spent days on end yearning for a cock to fill her while she watched him fucking the cowed and servile slave girl who functioned as his stable hand.

But Lightning tried not to think of the future. Ponygirls lived only in the present. This afternoon's workout had been particularly strenuous. It had rained during lunch and her thighs and legs were splattered with the mud of the track as she was led to the barn. Her back burned with the kisses of the whip she had received. She was being led back to the barn by a stable boy. He had attached a leash to the ring in her nose and she was following behind him dutifully, her useless arms locked behind her. Her vision of what was going on around her was severely limited by her blue neoprene hood. All of a sudden, she saw the form of the owner's daughter, her rival for the love of her trainer, loom up in front of her.

Anya had been waiting for the ponygirl to be brought down from the training track to the barn. She had something special planned for the beast today. She had sat for an hour by the barn door bullshitting with the hands, teasing them about their use of the blue hooded, faceless ponies. She had fingered a couple of them to orgasm to the delight of the small crowd that had gathered around her. They were like toys to her. The smooth, blue neoprene which covered their faces and heads did indeed deprive them of all humanity. She hardly believed that she had let Drabik make her wear one, even though it had excited her beyond words when she had seen herself in it.

So she recognized Lightning, not by her face, which was blue and featureless like all of the other ponies, but by her physical self, her shape, her walk, the size and form of her breasts. When the mud spattered pony had come close enough, she read the tattooed blue letters above her swaying breasts, demarking her as '*Molnya*'.

She waved the stable boy who was leading Lightning to a halt and approached the surprised pony. She stood in front of her until she was sure, by the shudder that ran visibly through the animal, that the pony had seen her. This was to be a special moment.

"So here's the ponygirl champion," she announced in Russian to the stable hands. "She doesn't look like much right now, does she?" She pointed to Lightning's brown spattered legs. She took hold of the leash from the stable boy and pulled the pony close to her. There was a round of laughter from the small crowd.

"But she does have nice tits," Anya remarked. She grabbed Lightning's right breast and squeezed it hard, causing the pony to mew from behind her bit.

Lightning was frightened. She remembered well her last encounter with the owner's daughter. To see her now portended unhappiness and abuse. If there was one good thing about racing season, it was that she would be out of the cruel woman's reach for many weeks. She could not understand the harsh sounding words being used by the young woman, but she knew from the laughter that she had been the butt of a joke.

Lightning recognized, by voice or face, the young men who were standing around the pony barn door. All of them had used her at one time or another. It was funny how in private the men could be such passionate and almost tender lovers while in public the most callous and brutal.

Anya took hold of the ring on Lightning's collar and paraded her around the circle of men. "Who would like to fuck the ponygirl champion?" she said tauntingly. "Who has the biggest cock here?"

The men laughed, their merriment toned down a bit by the prospect of having their cocks measured against one another's. Supposedly, size didn't matter, but you could never convince men of that.

A tall, broad shouldered, blond youth stood out from the small crowd. He wore a white, peasant style shirt and dirty, black blue jeans. His hair was stringy and long and he had a full, bushy beard. He had large, strong hands, big as platters. He looked around the assembly of young men disdainfully. Unembarrassed, he reached inside his pants and pulled out a tumescent, 7" long, thick digit with a large rounded head. "I'll put my cock up against anyone's," he said disdainfully.

Anya took a look at the long, thick, flaccid meat. She smiled and said brazenly, "It doesn't count unless it's hard." The men all laughed.

"Let's get the ponygirl to help you out," she said. She gave Lightning the hand signal that required her to fall to her knees and the ponygirl obeyed instantly. She saw the soft male tissue in front of her and knew without need for explanation what was required. She also knew that all of the eyes of the men were on her. She felt the straps to her bit being removed and the steel contrivance withdrawn from her mouth. Her head was tilted slightly upwards from her pony collar and her mouth was poised to receive the man's tool. She opened her mouth dutifully and engulfed the already swelling prick.

Lightning tried to ignore the catcalls of the men as she performed her task diligently. But she could not ignore the sound of the woman's voice as she laughed and joked with the men. What turn of fate had determined that she should be on her knees in the mud, naked and bound, all of her will and dignity taken away while this woman should be free, free to laugh, free to determine her own destiny? Lightning had thought herself beyond humiliation. Everything that could be done to her had been done and in every situation. But the taunting sound of the mistress's voice tore into her like a knife. It reminded her of who she was and who she could have been. She thought back to a night many months ago on a lonely, dark road in

Tennessee where she had spoken her last free words, virtually the last words she had ever spoken. She had thought a thousand times since then of how she should have run away, done something. She still remembered her sense of fearful surprise when the cloth had descended over her face and her mind had begun to fog.

Lightning applied her lips and skillful tongue to the man's meat. The cock had hardened and it was difficult to apply herself to its whole length. She began to let the heat and taste of the fleshly sword to comfort her, ignite her own need. She shut out her thoughts of the woman, the crowd around her and her past, and concentrated in bringing pleasure to the master. It was the only control over them that she ever had, the ability to administer pleasure to them through her mouth, the only means of expression she had. She was pleased when she heard the man moan. She had control of him.

Suddenly, Lightning felt her head pulled backwards. Anya had taken hold of her long, chestnut colored ponytail and forced her to give up the man's prick.

"Let's take a look!" Anya exclaimed. The man proudly displayed his manhood in its ultimate rampant state. It had gained a full two inches and was red and swollen. Lightning's juices dripped off of it. Anya turned to the growing crowd of men. "Is this the best you can do?" she challenged them laughingly. The woman had no modesty where sex was concerned. It had been around her all her life. When slave girls and ponygirls could be fucked anytime anywhere and anyplace, often right out in the open, certain delicacies of a teenaged young woman were cast aside.

The big man beamed with pride at his displayed virility. Anya was about to name him the champ when a voice called out from the gallery. "Not so fast, Anya. I think I can do better than that."

It was a lean, wiry fellow with dark hair and a clean shaven face. He wore a little hat, somewhat like a fedora on his head which was crumpled and dirty. He had on a denim work shirt and blue jeans over high work boots. He smiled wryly as he stepped into the circle that had formed around the ponygirl.

Without fanfare, he undid his fly and produced a long, skinny cock with an uncircumcised head. It was sleek and he shook it like a hose.

Anya gazed on it with approval. "Well, it's long enough, but it looks kind of skinny."

"Just give me a minute," the laconic man said. "Get the slut over here."

Anya, enjoying every minute of the ponygirl's humiliation, dragged her over by her tail to where the man stood. Lightning had to scramble on her knees, smearing more mud on her legs. Her arms strained behind her in their confines to help her keep her balance, something that she did still automatically even though it had been months since she had actually used them. When her mouth was presented to the snake-like cock belonging to the skinny man, she opened her lips and took it in.

Sucking an uncircumcised cock was somewhat different than sucking one on which the foreskin had been removed. The skin inside the flesh that slid back exposing the cock's tip was more sensitive and delicate. But it produced a more satisfying reaction in its owner when she massaged it with her tongue. There was no knob on the end to circle her lips around. But all in all, the warmth of her mouth and the assiduous workings of her tongue had the same reaction.

Lightning could feel the man's cock growing in her mouth as she pleasured it. Anya pressed against the back of her head and the tip of the prick slid into her throat. Lightning began to gasp and choke at the sudden filling of her air passageway. She struggled to free herself, but the woman had a firm grasp on the hair behind her blue clad head. She held her there for a full minute and then pulled her head back so that the cock sprang free of her lips.

Anya gave Lightning's face a sharp slap. "Don't be sloppy ponygirl," she called out in Russian. There was more laughter at her joke. Lightning cringed in misery at the sound of her cruel laugh and the appreciation that the men showed for her degradation of her.

"Open up, *Molnya*, suck the nice man's cock!" Anya ordered in Russian, her pleasure at the pony's unhappiness evident. She pushed the head forward again and Lightning, the thought of disobedience or resistance never crossing her mind, reopened her lips to receive the hot meat.

The ponygirl worked on the now bulging cock for at least another minute. The man had placed his hands on either side of her face and was guiding her movements. His back arched and gave out a sigh as the wet warmth of Lightning's mouth sent waves of pleasure through him. Lightning felt her head jerked back again. She had wanted to make the man come, gain the admiration of the crowd for her skills, bring an end to her torment. She gave a little whine.

Anya released the head of the ponygirl and stepped up to the two men. The big man's cock was still rampant and hard and he held it in his hand stroking it. The skinny man's cock had indeed fattened and lengthened as a result of Lightning's attention to it. The two men stood side by side proudly exhibiting their weapons. Anya looked down at the two stiff pricks. "I don't know," she called out to the others. "I can't tell which is bigger." She looked up into the eyes of the two men. "I'll have to feel them for myself," she announced.

The beautiful, young gangster's daughter took possession of the men's meat with her two hands. Her audacity discomforted the two men, but the crowd loved it. Their eyes oscillated between the points of contact of her hands on the two men's dicks and her own tantalizing breasts, her firm ass, her long legs. No one fucked the beautiful gangster's daughter, but there was not a one who would not have liked to try.

Suddenly, Anya had made her decision. She released the big man's cock and pulled the skinny man towards the crowd by his meat. "I pronounce this as the best cock on the estate!" she called out. The men gave a hearty cheer. The blond man had a disconcerted look on his face. Anya reached for his meat again and pulled him towards her with it. "And this one's not bad either!" The men all cheered again and the blond man seemed comforted.

The black haired girl announced that the skinny man would have the honor of fucking the ponygirl champion. A stanchion was rolled out of the barn and set up in the middle of the men. Lightning was pulled to her feet by her hair and pushed over it. She felt her legs spread wide and her boots tied off to the stanchion's feet, spreading her legs widely. She knew that she was about to get raped in front of all of the men and probably more than once. She was familiar with the tendencies of a crowd of aroused men. It was okay. She would endure it. But the presence of her enemy, the woman who hated her with seemingly all of her existence made her dismally unhappy.

The stanchion had a round padded top and Lightning's waist pressed against it. Her plump breasts dangled down below her as her collar was affixed to a ring in the stanchion's base. All that she could see was a tiny, round sample of the activity around her. She felt her bit being reapplied to her mouth and tied off behind her head. She felt a hard, rough hand on her naked buttocks and another one begin to tease her already moistened slit between her nether lips.

Anya took a spot in front of the ponygirl. From somewhere she had obtained a thin, leather riding crop. She waved it into the air. "Who thinks that I should warm up the beast for our well endowed friend?" she called out. A roar of approval followed. Anya waved the wand and called for silence. "Let's hear the slut scream," she said. Anya's face was fevered with her own lust. This was going better than she thought. She could sense the misery being experienced by the ponygirl and she reveled in it. The men had grown silent and she showed the whip to the ponygirl. Lightning saw the whip and then looked up at the shapely young woman's cruel face, into her eyes. It was the same look that she had given Lightning out in the forest a week ago. Lightning moaned in desperation. She hated to be whipped, would never get used to it.

Anya disappeared from her view. There was a moment's pause. And then the lash struck across her buttocks like a tongue of fire. Lightning screeched through her bit at the pain. Another blow and than another landed across the plump cheeks of her ass. Her hands writhed in her bonds behind her back and she moved her hips futilely in an effort to avoid the blows. The men stood around silenced and compelled by the cruel spectacle. Lightning shook her faceless blue head and moaned and cried.

Anya was in seventh heaven as she lacerated the buttocks of the despised ponygirl. Ten excruciating blows in all she gave her, enjoying every one. The pony screamed and made agonized, mumbled pleas through the steel bit in her mouth. The places where the pony had been struck were marked by ten bright red lines of red.

Anya put down the whip, her fancy, white, silk blouse matted with her sweat. The outlines of her breasts and her lacey bra could be seen beneath it. Men leered at her longingly. She motioned to the lanky man with the big cock. "She's all yours, comrade," she said mockingly. She watched as the man stepped between the slut's wide spread thighs. She saw the head of the sleek, thick instrument pry apart the hairless nether lips. The pony was wet with her own lust, and the cock slid easily home.

Feeling the man's long, thick meat press between her lower lips, Lightning gave a sigh of both frustration and relief. Her whipping was over, but now she would have to endure the stoking of her lust. Once her thighs had been spread wide, Lightning's habitual need for sexual stimulation took over. Knowing that soon a hot, rigid male member would penetrate her made her loins begin to burn. Not even the whipping could impede the growth of her passion. She didn't care what the men saw. Most, if not all of them, had fucked her before. But it was the woman's presence that disturbed her. She would see her base, animal lust displayed, watch her shudder and jerk as her orgasm overtook her and prove her for the slut and the whore that she had become.

Anya came back around to the front of the splayed ponygirl. She leaned over and grabbed one of her breasts, tugging and playing at the nipple. The man had started sawing his meaty weapon inside her and the pony was responding to her assault with small moans and heavy breath. Anya moved her head close to the pony's ear. "Come for me, little ponygirl," she whispered in English. "Come like the slut that you are. I promised you that I would see you again. And I have such a special surprise for you. But for now, let the men see you come. They'll all want to fuck you later. Won't that be nice?"

Lightning groaned in hatred and pleasure as she was driven inexorably to the summit of her passion. The man had his strong hands on her hips and he plunged back and forth ruthlessly, gliding his cock across her pleasure bud, rasping along the walls of her pussy. She heard the cruel words of the black haired mistress and felt her fingers teasing her stiff, burning nipple.

The man behind her had stamina and was holding back his completion until he heard the ponygirl begin hers. Lightning felt her blood running hotter and hotter. As she began a rhythmic whine, each high note corresponding to the man's deep thrust within her, the men around her began to become excited all over again. They began to clap in unison with her exclamations of pleasure. The ponygirl's mind became clouded, all thoughts were brushed aside except for the intense need to reach her peak. She tried to match the man's thrusts, but had no leverage. Her breasts swayed frantically beneath her. When her lust crested and her pussy began to contract and spasm with mind wrenching pleasure, she moaned her body's ecstasy loudly and began to shiver and shake. She felt her head yanked back and her eyes met the probing, spiteful eyes of her rival. "Ooooooooooh!" she cried out in pleasure and misery. "Ohhhhhhhhhhh!"

She felt the man's cock spurt his hot load deep within her and her orgasm rose another notch. "Ohhhhhhhhh! Ohhhhhhhhhhh!" She had jammed her eyes closed and was thankful, for once, that her face was hidden from the other woman's prying eyes. "Ohhhhhhh! Ohhhhhhhhhh!" she called out. She wanted the pleasure to go on forever, to carry her away, to drown out all consciousness for all time. But when the man's efforts began to subside as his tool and balls were drained of their essence, Lightning began to recover her own sensibilities. She was breathing as heavily as if she had just finished a long, intense workout. Her whole body felt limp and tired. She opened her eyes to see the applauding men and the widespread grin of satisfaction on the Russian woman.

"And, now," Anya called out, "the second prize." The tall, broad shouldered, blond haired man had not put away his piece. He had been stroking it intently as he had watched the other man drill the pony's hot, little pussy. He perked up when he heard Anya's voice. It was silly really. He could fuck the ponygirl *Molnya* almost any time that he wanted. But he never wanted to more than now. He might have been second, but he would make her scream louder.

Anya came back behind the still recovering pony and placed her pale, white hands on the pony's buttocks, drawing open the cheeks so that the delicate brown flower of her anus was open to view. "Here's the hole for second place," she announced. The blond man nodded. He loved to fuck the ponies in the ass. She would really feel his cock now.

Lightning heard, but did not understand, Anya's cries, except as they were an enticement for more use of her body. She stiffened when she felt Anya part her rear cheeks. She was unhappy, but not surprised when she felt a thick, hard cock press against that small opening.

She had become somewhat enamored of ass fucking herself over the months and she was able to relax her muscles and widen the point of entry to her bowels. But this man was thick. Despite her willingness to cooperate, she felt the delicate tissue surrounding the brown star begin to stretch and tear. She moaned with pain as the man pressed himself deeply within her, the dryness of his cock burning her. But when he had moistened his prick on her innards, the going got better and she sighed with pleasure as the meat glided back and forth through the tight ring of her ass.

Because of his higher target, the man was forced to lean over the bent over pony and his chest pressed against Lightning's back, his hard belly crushing her vestigial fingers and hands. He took long, leisurely strokes that made the pony's toes curl and her eyes roll back into her head. Her passions were still burning when the other man's cock had left her and her lust quickly started to build. The man's pace was agonizing to her. She felt the large tube of hot flesh drag slowly back, tormenting the sensitive entrance and then push slowly back deep within her, filling her, making her moan. He snaked his hands around her chest and took possession of her dangling breasts. He massaged them and teased them, squeezing and pulling at her rigid nipples, cupping the large mounds in his huge hands.

She felt a hand patting her face and opened her eyes to see the face of her chief tormentor, Anya, smiling at her. The other men had grown silent again and only Lightning's frustrated groans could be heard. All of a sudden, she began to rebel against her cruel and demeaning predicament. It isn't fair, it isn't right, her mind screamed. "I don't want to be a ponygirl! I don't want to be a slut! Leave me alone, please, please! Let me go, please!" Her mind was awash in misery as she felt the relentless cock continue to stoke her passion. Her mind might have been rebelling, but her body had its own needs, needs ruthlessly imbued to it by months and months of training.

Lightning squeezed her rectal muscles tightly, mindlessly hoping to somehow expel the thick, steel hard invader. She shook her back and torso to try and knock the huge man off her. She arched her back to try and pull her blood filled, heavy breasts out of his reach. But the effort was in vain. It only excited the small crowd of men who had surrounded her and amused the horrible woman who had prompted this lascivious ordeal.

And the cock inside her continued to methodically stimulate her sensitive anal ring. Subtlety, almost without her knowledge, her physical needs began to outstrip her desire for liberation and an end to her humiliation. She wanted her lust to stop, but couldn't stop it, wanted her passion to subside, but couldn't quench it. She gave out a long, plaintive wail, "Oooooooooooooooooooou!" as she felt the familiar electricity in her womb that denoted her impending orgasm. She tried to fight it off, wish it away, but it continued to grow and grow within her as the cock insistently plundered her bowls and the man's hands teased and prodded her breasts. "Oooooooooouu! Oooooooooouuu!" Lightning called out as her pussy began to convulse and throb. She could feel her juices leaking from her like a torrent as she came and came. "Ahhhhhhhhhhhhh! Ahhhhhhhhhhhh!" she yelled as her whole body cramped and twisted in her pleasure. The man looked up at his confreres and smiled. He had made her cry out louder. He might have a smaller cock, not by much, but he was certainly the better cocksman. He had just begun to make her come.

The man's energies picked up as Lightning writhed beneath him. He increased the tempo of his thrust, now pounding his loins into the hard, muscled buttocks of the pony. Lightning's torment began again as her orgasm began anew.

Anya watched the ponygirl's explosive reaction to her ass fucking with satisfaction. She was just an animal. She had no right to Drabik's passions. Soon, like the other ponygirls, she would be in the hands of her drivers, unavailable to torment even by her, the owner's daughter. But Anya took consolation that Lightning's driver was one of the most vicious and cruel of all, second, if to anyone, only to his dwarfish brother.

In the end, after the blond giant had come and Lightning lay exhausted, draped across the stanchion, the crowd began to dissipate. After all, they had work to do. They were all horny and edgy and there were other ponygirls to fuck. Almost immediately, the men began to argue among themselves as to who was the better cocksman, the big blond giant, or the lanky, uncircumsized man who had fucked the pony first. Some men said that the blond man had had the advantage since Fiodor, the lanky man, had stoked her fires. Others said that Danya had had the harder task of making her come from her ass. And then there was the fact that Danya had caressed her breasts. But didn't Anya caress them too? Should her participation have disqualified Fiodor? Maybe they should have the contest again under closely defined and regulated circumstances? And so on. The debate went on in various forms for many weeks until it was all but forgotten.

Now that the men had gone away, Anya had her real surprise for the distressed ponygirl. It was something she had waited a whole week for. While the ponygirl was recovering, Anya signaled to one of the men who had stayed. He quickly walked away. While waiting for him to return, Anya approached the bent over, blue headed ponygirl and whispered to her. "How was that, *Molnya*? You looked like you really enjoyed it. I'll bet that when you were younger you didn't know that you were a slut just waiting to happen. It doesn't matter who the cock belongs to, does it?"

Anya looked up as the noise of a truck drew closer. She turned back to her prisoner.

"Look, little ponygirl, here is my surprise. Look! Look!"

Lightning raised her head and peered in front of her. She could see little, but she finally made out the vision of a truck. It was backing up to the area close to the pony barn door. There was a horse trailer attached to the back. Lightning was familiar with the horse trailers. She had been brought here on one. During the racing season, her drivers had transported her from place to place on one, her ankles spread and hooked to the floor, her waist pressed up against a bar across the center. Her collar would be chained to the front of the trailer and she would be sped away to the various ponygirl meets. But racing had not begun. What did it mean? Was this the surprise? Suddenly only one thing could occur to the forlorn former woman. The evil one had sold her! She was being taken away! But to where? And to whom? She would never see her trainer again, never see her lover, Persephone! The ponygirl began to wail and cry. She tried to shake free of her confinements desperately. She would run and run and run! They would never catch her, never!

Anya leaned over again and began to stroke her blue clad head. "Oh, no, little *Molnya*, you haven't been sold. Don't worry. We are going to have great fun together. You'll see. It's another pony who has to go. Someone you know."

The driver had gone into the pony barn and he exited it with a blue hooded, naked ponygirl in tow. The eye flaps to her blue hood were closed and she wore a shield gag over her lips and chin, concealing the thick, leather plug that was in her mouth. On her belly, she wore the snarling, terrible, rampant yellow wolf that was the symbol of the Grobgy estate. Above her pendulous breasts, breasts that Lightning would have recognized anywhere, she wore, stenciled in three inch high Cyrillic letters the name

'Persephone'. It was Lightning's ponygirl lover who had been sold. She was going away forever. She would be trained to run for some other estate. Even if she and Lightning were ever to appear at the same racing meet, she would never see her, never get close to her.

Persephone had suffered terribly from the romp in the woods the week before with Lightning and Anya. But she had no idea what it was all about. She had no way to know of Lightning's special relationship with her trainer, Drabik, nor of Anya's jealous rage. She had quickly put it out of her mind as one of the random horrors to which she, as a ponygirl, was subject to. She had learned something about her lover, the pony they called *Molnya*: she could speak English. How often as they had lain intertwined in the ponygirl meadow or when *Molnya*'s trainer had let them caress each other on their rides together had she wanted to speak her love and appreciation to the other pony. They had trained together, they had suffered together. They loved each other.

The former American college student had no idea why they were taking her from the barn. She had been training all day as a back row pony in the four pony chaise. In the spring, she had ran as part of a pair, first with *Molnya* and then with a tall, brown tailed pony. Running as a foursome took some getting used to. It was strange to see the backs of the ponies in front of you, their naked buttocks, their long ponytails flashing. It occurred to her that it was just how the driver behind her saw her. But now, it was time for dinner. She should be in her stall, kneeling on the floor her head buried in her bowl. Maybe someone wanted to use her, she thought. Well a good fuck before dinner would be all right. It had been a long day. But then she heard the anguished screech of another ponygirl just a few steps away from her. Something was happening. Something bad! Why were her eye flaps down? What was it that she was not supposed to see? Her knees weakened and her stomach turned over. What could it be?

Persephone's frightened reaction could not be discerned from her facial expression since her face had long ago been hidden away. She could not ask a question since all speech by ponygirls was expressly forbidden, even if her mouth was not securely gagged. The man next to her had a firm grip on her otherwise useless left arm and his other hand on a chain that led to the large gold ring in her nose so she could not run away, assuming there was anywhere to run to. But what was happening?

Lightning saw her lover being brought from the barn and her whole being became a huge, agonized wound. This woman was going to leave her nothing! She was going to destroy her! She loved the other ponygirl with all of her heart. She hadn't seen her for a week, not since the incident in the forest, but she knew that she was around and that eventually she would see her. Her trainer would take them to the woods together where they could kiss each other and caress. She could nestle on her lover's breast, take her plump nipples in her mouth, hear her sigh with pleasure. But all that was going away. There would be no more Persephone. No more love.

Her love for Drabik and his love for her was different. Her former trainer loved her like a pet, a possession. And she loved and needed to be possessed and used by him. But Persephone was her equal. She had shared her torments. She knew what it was like to be made into an animal. She knew what it was to have everything human taken away from you. Their flesh had melded, their souls touched, and all without one word being spoken between them and never having seen each other's faces.

Something broke in Lightning as she watched her lover being mounted into the pony trailer. She saw the pony struggling futilely as she was forced inside. Saw her back and buttocks as the man stepped down once she had been affixed within. She heard the truck's engine roar to life and watched as the trailer began to move, slowly at first, then faster, and then disappear to her left.

The pony hung her head and cried. Why had this woman done this? She had no choice but to submit to her trainer. She could refuse him nothing. She wanted and needed him, yes, but she had not stolen him. How could she, a dehumanized female with no face, no voice, compete with the black haired woman's feminine wiles and charms? Deep sobs wracked her chest, her eyes flooded with tears.

Anya watched, satisfied.

* * * * * * * * * * * * * *

Jake watched while Tucker unhitched the two blond ponies and gave them both a good rubdown. He had never seen the hard man like this. His strong hands kneaded the ponies' muscles tenderly from the tips of their toes to their necks. Jake had apologized to the broad shouldered, stone faced man for bringing the ponies back late. Tucker had shrugged it off and told Jake not to worry. Although Dora and Flora were a matched pair, they still had separate stalls and so they were isolated for their feedings. Jake agreed to help out with Flora, who was the slightly bigger of the two, and waited until she had slurped up the high protein concoction in her bowl. When she was done, as Tucker had instructed him, he had her stand over the drain and washed her body down with a hose. There was a sponge and soap and Jake washed every inch of the silent, docile pony. Her flesh was soft although her muscles were hard. Jake took pleasure in handling her plump, heavy orbs. He shampooed the long, blond tail that emanated from her hood and brushed it free of knots. When she was rinsed off, he knelt her down facing away from him, as Tucker had shown him, and removed the black neoprene hood so that he could wash her face

Rubbing a soft soapy cloth over the ponygirl's face from behind, Jake wondered how long it had been since the pony or anyone else had seen it. Flora seemed to enjoy his gentle massage of her facial muscles as he rubbed in a moisturizing cream. He applied the same cream to her shaved, pale head. The skin on her scalp was so pale that it was almost ghostly. It hadn't seen the sun for more than seven years. Jake asked himself the question that he had never asked anyone else for fear of the answer. Where did the older, used up ponies go? What was their ultimate fate? No one seemed to want to talk about it. How long before this thirty or so year old former woman have before she was cast aside? Was there a retiree home for ponygirls past their prime?

He decided that the question was not worth answering. Whatever this delightful pony's fate was, it was no business of his. He did not make this world and it was doubtful that he alone could do anything to change it.

After reinstalling the black hood, Jake had the pony stand and installed her against the long rail that bisected the stall. He tied off her boots about two feet apart and connected her nose ring via a chain to a hook in the wall in front of her. Before passing back under the bar again, Jake took a look at the serene appearance of the big, blond pony. Was her mind as empty as it appeared? Was there a whirlwind of thought and emotions circling inside unable to come out? Or had all humanity really be driven from this pleasant, pleasure giving female? He dipped under the rail and came behind the pony. He slapped her on her rump and left the stall, the swinging door banging behind him. As he passed Dora's stall, he could hear Tucker inside bringing the pony to orgasm.

He needed to go back to the carriage house where he and his boys lived but wanted to stop at the tack shop first. The tack shop was where all of the impedimenta of female slavery was stored. There was a party going on in the barracks and he could hear music, men's laughter and a girl's screams as he passed it. The sun had completely fallen now and spotlights spilled out over the lawn all around the grounds. The track was dark and quiet. It had little orange lights, about a hundred feet apart, mounted on the top of the rails and they made a strange glow all around it.

Jake retrieved his object at the tack shop and headed to the carriage house. When he reached it, he saw that workmen had already covered up the windows of the kitchen that he had smashed. The kitchen had been cleaned up and Martinez, Curley and Leon were sitting around the table morosely. Three slave girls stood like statutes in three corners of the room. Jake had no words for any of them and he went upstairs to his bedroom without speaking.

In the corner of his room, scrunched into the little cage that was bolted into the floor, was the American slave girl, Dana. She was still wearing the sheath like gag over her mouth and chin and had her hands bound behind her. She looked up at him with fear when he flicked on the lights.

The fixer/bodyguard failed to acknowledge the unhappy creature. He threw his package on the bed and stripped off his clothes. He wanted a good shower more than anything. A shower all alone.

The hot water was comforting as it poured over his head and body. He cleaned his body thoroughly and washed his short, brown hair. He thought of shaving, but rejected that thought. He had no desire to see himself in the mirror. He might not like what he saw.

It had been a long day and a long four day trip with Burnham and he wanted to get some sleep. But there was one duty he had promised himself he would perform before he slept. Still naked, he opened the cage for the slave girl and ordered her out. The girl obeyed without hesitation. Jake took her to the bathroom and let her empty her bladder and then, releasing her gag, he gave her a long drink of water from the sink.

Having brought the slave girl back into the bedroom, Jake looked up at the ceiling and found what he was looking for. The bedroom was large and there was a four foot square area free of any furniture or obstruction in front of the bed. He released the black haired slave girl's hands from behind her back and joined them in front. Leaving her standing there, he stepped over to the bed and opened his package from the tack shop. He drew out a two foot long, thin, steel chain with clips at both ends. He clipped one end to the girl's locked bracelets and the other to the small ring in the ceiling above her head. Her hands were raised above her, although not so high that she didn't have a firm footing on the floor. He went back to the bed and retrieved a three foot long, leather whip.

There had been no whips in the carriage house, but there was one now. For too long, Jake had decided, he had played by his own rules here in Kalikastan. He had thought himself above the cruelties and injustices that abided in this lawless nation. If he were going to survive here, he would have to play the game their way. And so would his men. He had fallen in love with a slave girl. He never would again.

The girl's lips were trembling and her eyes were watering when Jake turned back to her. She knew why her hands had been raise above her. She had seen Jake's fit of destructive anger when they had arrived at the carriage house earlier in the day. She had no delusions about her role in Kalikastan, Jake thought as he studied her frailty. And neither should he.

Jake reared back with the whip and gave the slave girl a fearsome blow across her pretty breasts. The girl screamed with pain. Jake waited for her voice to go silent and then he struck her again. Her wail of pain resounded throughout the house. Downstairs, Jake's men cringed as they heard the results of their boss's torture of the pretty, new slave girl. And so did the other slave girls who were getting the message that would soon be spread among their sisters: the carriage house was no longer a safe haven from pain and cruelty.

The strong, cold killer worked his way down the slave girl's body. He marked her belly, her thighs and her shins. Fierce red lacerations appeared wherever the whip landed. The girl screamed and moaned as she was assaulted, sagging in her bonds. When Jake was satisfied with his work on her front, he went to work on her back. As the whip began to tear the skin on her back, the slave girl began to plead and beg for mercy. Jake couldn't hear her. He was in a zone which he had usually reserved for the most dreadful tasks that he had carried out in his prolonged career. That the girl was innocent of any wrongdoing didn't matter to him. That she was young and pretty and willing to satisfy his every desire without any need to resort to brutalization didn't matter. What mattered was the lesson that Jake was teaching her, the men and slaves downstairs and especially himself. Fate had taken a hand in all of their lives. It had made some of them slaves and some of them masters. Slaves could not be slaves if the masters were not masters. And he was a master.

The girl was blubbering hysterically by the time Jake had finished. He threw the whip on the floor and went to the bathroom to get himself a drink of water. His lust was on him. Not the lust that had propelled him into Klara's arms every night, but a cold, cruel lust that needed anonymous, immediate fulfillment.

He stepped behind the red striped body of his slave girl, his property, and he ran his hands over her graceful, full back. He reached around her and grabbed her pained breasts and squeezed them until the girl moaned. He placed his hand between her legs and covered her naked mons with his hand. She was his, but she was just property. As he used the ponygirls for his pleasure, he would use her. He would not care how she felt, what she wanted, whether she loved him. She would fulfill her role or suffer. And suffer anyway if that was his want.

It was his desire now that she open herself to him, that she ignite her bodily passions for his enjoyment. He slid his finger between the girl's bald, sweaty nether lips and stroked the crease of her cleft. Despite her misery, the girl spread her legs obediently and pushed her cunt against him. Her training was at work. She had been beaten by cruel and inhumane men before and had been ordered to perform for them. She knew now that a failure to perform would cause immediate additional miseries to be drawn down upon her. The American slave girl, Dana, closed her eyes and brought herself to that special place that she needed to loosen the bonds on her lust.

Dana had not had many really lustful experiences with boys or men when she went off to the University of Illinois last year. She had joined the woman's field hockey team and had met a young girl, Linda, with whom she had struck up an immediate and warm friendship. They were both psych majors and they spent almost all of their time together. One night, when Dana's roommates were away for the weekend, the girls had brought some pizza and beers back to Dana's dorm room. They watched a tearjerker movie and drank up the six pack. It was late and, when the credits finally rolled to a finish on the small TV screen, there was utter silence in the room. Dana looked over at her pretty, blond friend. She had never had lustful desires for women, but her desire for Linda's lips seemed so right. Linda seemed to think so too as she edged herself closer to her black haired friend and wrapped her arm around her shoulders.

"Dana..." she started to say.

Dana placed her finger on the other girl's lips and leaned towards her. She replaced her finger with her soft, burning lips and kissed the pretty blond haired girl. Linda opened her lips willingly and Dana's tongue slid inside. They kissed for fifteen minutes without a break. Then they hugged each other and cried. And then they kissed again. Dana couldn't remember whose idea it was to go to the bedroom, but they found themselves on her narrow bed naked, their hot skin stoking each other's passions.

Neither of the girls had had a lesbian encounter before and so they experimented hesitatingly on each other. Dana remembered the first time that she took Linda's breast in her mouth; her head swam with lust. And when she felt the gentle, probing fingers of Linda's right hand on her soft, moistened slit, she sighed with passion.

Dana and Linda had been taken together. Their affair had continued throughout the fall and winter semesters. During spring break they had decided to join the other thousands of college kids in their annual migration to Florida. They had spent the days sunbathing in their bikinis and their evenings drinking in the beach bars. On the third night there, someone who had taken note of their charms had followed them back to their hotel room. Dana awoke to find a foul smelling cloth pressed over her face and the sound of Linda's muffled cry for help. All had gone black. She had never seen her lover Linda again.

So it was Linda's loving hand that she imagined now as Jake pressed her nether lips apart, Linda's finger that she imagined exploring her crevasse, teasing the point of her clitoris, her hand holding and caressing her breast. She lubricated quickly, as she had been trained to do, and let her lusts build.

Jake was not interested in the whore's pleasure per se. But he wanted her lust to accelerate his. He pressed his thick, hard cock in the valley between her nether cheeks as he teased his slave's body into responsiveness. When his hand was covered with her moisture, he reached back and spread it over the tip of his rampant cock. He spread the girl's firm, rear globes apart and sought the little brown star between them with the head of his prick.

Dana gasped as she felt its intrusion and then let her rectal muscles relax to receive her master's cock. Her trainers had quickly taught her to enjoy the use of her nether hole and her already ignited passion was driven higher by the feel of the fat cock entering her. She squeezed the tool with her rear opening as it slipped within her, giving her user maximum pleasure, as she had been taught. She moaned when she felt her possessor's manhood bury itself in her bowels to the hilt.

The heat of the slave girl's bowels gave Jake a surge of pleasure. He grasped her breasts tightly and began to saw himself across the delicate tissue around her rear opening. He took her nipples in his fingers and pinched and twisted them while his lust grew higher and higher. He felt the girl rocking to meet his thrusts and he heard her breath thicken.

Dana gave a little cry when her orgasm began. When Jake heard her passionate exclamation and felt her body begin to quiver and shake in his arms, his lust overboiled and he shot his hot load deeply inside her. He grunted and groaned at each throb of pleasure that passed through him. The girl was rocking and moaning, squeezing her buttocks tightly together to capture the cock that had sent her over the edge.

Jake leaned against the girl, his forces spent. He let himself soften within her and then withdrew his flaccid meat. He went to the washroom and cleaned himself. When he returned, he looked at the anxious, still flushed face of his property. He had not fucked her on the trip back from Dlitski to Burnham's estate, having decided to use one of the new girls Burnham had bought instead. He was satisfied with her training and ability. She was pretty, passionate and obedient. She was a good slave, valuable property. But that's all that she would be.

Jake turned out the main light in the room and went to his bed. He left the slave girl standing naked at the foot, her arms raised up by the chain to the ceiling. He did not bother to gag her because, if she talked, he would just beat her. Jake crawled into bed and drew the satin sheet around him. He took a look at his new slave girl's face and saw her uncertainty and fear. He drew his eyes down her marred but delectable body. She would be there in the morning. He would use her again.

The end of Book 5

www.ingramcontent.com/pod-product-compliance
Lightning Source LLC
Chambersburg PA
CBHW020608250626
47154CB00004B/1412